ROCK THE LINE

A GRACEFALL ROCK STAR ROMANCE

VICTORIA ZAK

Sign up for Victoria Zak's newsletter on her website to
receive a free ebook copy of her
Guardians of Scotland novella
Highland Destiny

You'll also find additional special offers, bonus content and
info on new releases.

www.victoriazakromance.com
victoria@victoriazakromance.com

 facebook.com/VictoriaZakAuthor

bookbub.com/authors/victoria-zak

instagram.com/victoriazakromance

twitter.com/VictoriaZak2

Rock the Line: A Gracefall Rock Star Romance
Victoria Zak
Copyright 2021 by Victoria Zak

Cover Design by JAB Designs

ISBN: 978-1-942516-37-8

❀ Created with Vellum

This series is dedicated to the wild at heart. Rock on!

1

*L*ate again, Jake raced into the Tin Flask, a bar he co-owned with his older brother, Brian, who was totally going to give him shit for being late for his shift. But he didn't care, not today, for his life was about to change forever. His heart pounded, not from the two-block run to work, but from the exhilaration pulsing in his veins. Jake couldn't believe it. He'd gotten the call.

Catching his breath, he made his way to the back of the Tin Flask where his brother was drying a glass with a scowl on his face. Brian didn't say a word, but Jake would be lying on the floor if looks could kill. With one fuck-up after another, the glare had lost its effect over the years. Now, it was plain irritating. Christ, he was a grown man.

As Jake tied a black apron around his waist, he took a drink order from a blonde in a red dress. She flashed him a smile of bright red lipstick, and he winked with a lopsided grin. This typical back-and-forth flirting came naturally to Jake. But it always stopped there. He wasn't interested in hooking up with the women who went into the bar. They came with too much baggage.

With the devil in the blonde's eyes coupled with shooting whiskey, she was definitely looking for a good time. Too often he'd seen this scenario play out. It always ended in him throwing some overzealous dude out of the bar, leaving Jake to listen to the drunken female rant about how she hates men as they waited for a cab.

Jake stood next to his brother as he reached for a bottle of Jim Beam. "Sorry, I'm late."

Brian said nothing.

"I got the call." Saying it out loud felt damn good.

"Did you hear that?" Brian sarcastically said louder than needed in front of Sergeant Tom Calhoun of the Reno police, who had been Jake's late father's partner, and two off-duty cops, Dominic and Chris, who Jake had graduated with from the police academy five years ago. Even though he'd left the force, they'd remained friends. They were family. "Jake got the call." Brian glared at Jake.

"Which call? The one saying you're the father?" Dominic snickered while Chris joined in, humming Billie Jean.

"Didn't your mama warn you about breaking young girls' hearts?" Dominic never resisted an opportunity to bust his balls. It was his life goal.

"Real funny, asshole." Jake took the towel Brian was using and rat-tailed Dominic. "At least I get laid."

"Hell, I'd get laid, too, if I had rocker hair like yours," Dominic said, once again busting his balls.

"For the life of me, I don't understand why women like men with long hair." Tom shook his head, tossing back his beer. "Long-haired hippies," he grumbled.

Jake filled the blonde's shot glass, smiling at the old-fashioned comment that reminded him a lot of his dad. Age and years of law service had taken a toll on Tom, graying his hair and creating hard lines that creased his face. One more year and the big man would retire, just like his father would have. Hell, if his father were still alive, life would be different. Both he and his brother would still be wearing a badge. "Are you going to tell us, or am I going to have to find a mind reader?" Sergeant Calhoun wasn't one for bullshit.

A sheen of sweat covered Jake's forehead. Breaking the news that he was leaving the Tin Flask, the bar he and his brother opened in his father's honor wasn't going to be easy —especially for Brian. "I got the gig."

Tom looked at him as if he didn't understand English, Dominic stared with his mouth open, and Chris broke the silence. "Hell yeah, bro." He fist-bumped Jake.

Disappointed, Brian shook his head. Jake didn't need to guess what his brother was thinking. *Jake, the screwup.* But he was wrong this time. Being chosen to replace the great Moxley Sims from Gracefall was the opportunity of a lifetime. No more busting his ass at the bar to pay the bills. No more laying down guitar tracks in the studio for a band he'd never get credit for. Finally, he'd have a steady gig—a band he'd dreamed of since he was a kid. He'd be a part of something larger than life.

"What about the bar?" Brian asked while he crossed his arms over his chest. "I thought we were in this together."

A sequence of images from the day his father died played out before him like a tragic TV drama show. It started with him responding to a domestic violence call. Jake had arrived late. His body tensed as he recalled getting out of his police cruiser as he watched a man point a loaded gun at his dad. Gunfire had rung in his ears as he'd drawn his weapon and shot the guy dead, but it had been too late. It ended with his dad lying lifeless in his arms.

The tragic death had been a devastating blow to Jake's

family. For their mother and their own wellbeing, he and Brian had turned in their badges and become entrepreneurs. The men and women in blue had supported the Tin Flask throughout the years, making Jake's decision even more complex. He didn't want to let his family down, yet he couldn't throw away his one dream of being in a rock band. And Gracefall was at the top of their game. As tragic as losing a rock guitarist icon like Moxley Sims was, Jake's talent would only add to the band's success. He had an excellent ear for music and was a quick study; he could play anything from just listening to it. It's why he'd been so successful as a studio musician. And why Gracefall wanted him.

"This is classic Jake." Brian exhaled as he placed the glass he was drying on the shelf behind him.

"What's that supposed to mean?" Jake knew, but maybe this time his brother's reaction would be different.

The glare in Brian's eyes deepened. "Oh, I think you know."

"Well, boys." Tom's barstool skidded across the floor like a needle screeching across a record, silencing the room as he stood. "It's closing time."

Chris followed Tom's lead, but Dominic didn't move. He tossed back the rest of his beer. "Where's the popcorn? This is going to be good."

Tom slapped Dominic on the back of his head. "Idgit. Let's go."

Dominic winced. "Really, Tom?" He rubbed the back of his neck as he got up from his stool. "No need to get violent."

Jake wasn't surprised that the guys left. They'd already seen the shitshow and the reruns. He watched the door close behind them before addressing his brother. "So, you think I'm fucking up again." He crossed his arms, waiting for all hell to break loose.

"I don't think, I know."

"This time you're wrong."

"Am I?" Brian pinned him with a glare. "Should I remind you?"

"Do I have a choice?" No, he didn't. Throughout his whole life, Brian had called him out every chance he got.

"For starters, your grand idea of becoming a cop back-fired. You quit."

"I resigned, and you know why."

"No, Jake, it wasn't about dad's death. Your heart was never in it. You were always late, not giving a shit about anyone but yourself."

"That's not true," he lied. Well, it wasn't all a lie. His father had pressured him to be a cop to keep him out of trouble and convince him he needed a solid plan for the future that didn't involve rock and roll. His father's warnings were still embedded in his brain:

"Playing in a band won't pay the bills."

"I'm not holding your bail money."

"Get a real job."

"Don't do drugs."

It was no surprise that his father had a shit fit when Jake had dropped out of college to devote all his time to rock and roll. After one of his bandmates ended up behind bars and his band broke up, he decided his father was right. With his dreams of becoming a musician ending, he'd joined the police academy. No, it wasn't the path he'd wanted for himself, but there was no other choice for him at the time.

Brian continued down fuck-up memory lane. "Then remind me about your spontaneous trip to the altar in

Vegas? Tell me, have you heard from your wife? How's that working out?"

Now, that was a low blow and on point. Marrying Stacy in a chapel in Vegas hadn't been the brightest idea. But he'd fallen fast and hard; she was the real deal. Or so he thought. Jake had woken the next morning hungover from drunken marital bliss with Stacy gone. His world crashed and burned when he'd found the dreaded "it's not you but me" apology note claiming she needed space.

After the first six months of radio silence from Stacy, he should've filed for divorce. He knew it was over, but he couldn't accept being a failure—not again—so he held on to hope that one day she would come back. After a time, he'd plain forgotten about the whole deal. No need to keep reminding himself of another fuck-up.

Christ, what was he holding on to? Did he really think that she would come back? Stacy hadn't filed for divorce, so there had been hope. But she was also nowhere to be found. Maybe he held on to prove his brother wrong that his good intentions weren't always bad ideas.

"Okay, you might have a point there, but this time it's different. Being in a band has always been my dream. I've finally got a chance to do what I love."

"No, Jake, you're a thirty-year-old man chasing a fantasy."

Jake stood silent, fuming. Why couldn't his brother be happy for him? Why couldn't he see that this was the real deal?

"Have you signed a contract?"

"No. Management is flying me out to California to go over details."

"How about a lawyer? You'll need one to look over the

contract. Musicians get screwed out of tons of money because of poorly written contracts."

"I have one."

Brian crossed his arms and glared. "You haven't thoroughly thought this out, have you?"

His brother's accusations couldn't be further from the truth. He'd dealt with many contracts through all his years of studio experience and had a fantastic music attorney. Jake knew what he was doing, but Brian would never give him the satisfaction to recognize it.

"I told you, I have an attorney. How do you think deals are made in the studio?" He raised his brows, giving Brian a second to answer. "That's right, you don't, and you've never taken the time to ask me. In fact, when was the last time you stopped by the studio? I've invited you."

"Someone has to run the bar." Brian retreated his harsh tone. "You sure as hell don't have an interest."

Now, there was an idea, for once, that hadn't been Jake's. It was Brian's idea to open a bar in their father's name where all the local cops could hang out. So, how was Jake to say no when the Tin Flask was in honor of their dad?

"I told you my main focus was music."

Frustrated, Brian shook his head. "I just—"

"Just what? Didn't believe me? For once in my life, I'm going to do what I want. I'm done trying to please people. It would be nice to have your support."

Brian's demeanor softened. "You have my support. I just don't want to see one of your good intentions turn into another bad idea."

"Hell, I'm not afraid to take a chance and step on my dick."

"Oh, I know. I know." The brothers laughed.

"So, when do you leave for California?" Brian asked as he turned toward the liquor shelf behind him.

"I'm flying out tomorrow afternoon."

Brian returned with a bottle of whiskey and two shot glasses. "Good. I'll drive you to the airport." He poured them both a shot, then handed one to Jake. "Here's to not fucking up." They clinked glasses

Jake didn't know if Brian was sincere or if they were prematurely celebrating another fuck-up.

"Here's to living the dream."

2

*J*ake arrived in California with a warm welcome from a personal driver provided by Gracefall, who then drove him to the Sunset Plaza Hotel, where he'd be staying for the next couple of days. The hotel didn't look like anything special from the outside, but inside it was all Hollywood. They had set him up in a swanky city-view suite with a balcony and king-size bed. Everything had a European style, from the gold and neutral color palette on the walls to the furniture. In all the times he'd been to California to do studio work at Clef Tonic Records, they had never set him up like this.

After checking into his room and settling in, Jake had just enough time to call for room service, shower, and get ready for his meeting with Gracefall at The Black Veil across the street. In the lobby, he'd seen a flyer for an all-female Ozzy Osborne tribute band, Crazy Bitches, advertising their show tonight at The Black Veil before his meeting. He'd be checking that out for sure.

Feeling damn good about tonight, Jake left the plaza and headed to the nightclub. The sun was setting behind the mountains, casting an orange hue across the sky like it was on fire. Cars cruised The Strip at a steady pace as he waited to cross the street to the club.

He stood in awe at the historic rock and roll building. For the last fifty years, the hole-in-the-wall nightclub sat on the corner of an intersection known as Big Time Street and Broken Dreams Boulevard. Back in the day, it had launched many musicians' careers and destroyed others. As he looked at the four-lane street, it was clear that The Black Veil had been a crossroad for many bands. Either you had the drive or didn't. There was no easy way in—artists had paid their dues, battled the competition. If a band had sold out at The Black Veil, a record deal was sure to follow. If not, they kept chasing the dream until they had to go back to working a nine-to-five. Jake felt like one of the lucky ones.

Jake passed the long line of people waiting to get into the nightclub and walked up to one of the bouncers, who looked mean and big and ready to kick his ass. He flashed his pass, which had been left for him at the front desk of the hotel. The bouncer gave him a once-over, then nodded and lifted the red velvet rope. A group of women yelled out in disapproval as he walked toward the door. He just smiled and shook his head in disbelief. Rock star perks were kickass.

Inside, the place was packed and rocking out to Crazy Bitches, who were playing their version of "Crazy Babies" on stage. Well, he assumed it was Crazy Bitches because he couldn't see past the crowd to confirm. Whoever was shredding the guitar solo was killing it.

Jake shouldered his way across the floor to the stairs, which led to a second level and a better view of the stage. At the top of the stairs, another red velvet rope and another bouncer restricted access to the upper level.

"Private party up here tonight," the bouncer announced as he crossed his arms over his thick chest, sending out a "don't fuck with me" vibe. Jake wasn't intimidated. He'd dealt with far more dangerous dudes than then this guy when on the police force.

"I have a pass." He flashed the bouncer his pass and hoped it was good enough to get through. Why not? It had gotten him in the club.

"What's your name?" the bouncer asked as he turned to the table next to him, looking over a list of names.

"Jake Quin."

The bouncer found his name, and his demeanor changed. "You're good to go, Mr. Quin." He lifted the rope and let him in.

He was really getting used to these rock star perks.

Jake found a standing spot behind the wrought-iron railing, giving him a full view of the stage. The lead singer's long black hair bounced up and down as she banged her head with the crowd. Her supercharged stage performance had everyone from the first row to the back of the club singing and pumping their fists in the air.

It had only been a week since he'd been on that same stage auditioning for Gracefall's lead guitarist position. He'd almost ruined his chance when he arrived at the audition wearing an eighties-style fringe leather jacket. His costume plan to wear something that would make him stand out was an epic fail and almost cost him the audition. The band tried to kick him out of the club without even hearing him play. With only seconds to do damage control, he'd lost the jacket and nailed his guitar solo, impressing Gracefall. Who knew? Fringe was a hard no.

As the next song began, the spotlight shined on the lead

guitarist. Jake's breath lodged in his throat when he recognized the blonde-haired beauty.

Holy shit! Elliot Phoenix!

Jake didn't know her personally. However, he felt like he did since he'd been following her on social media for the past year. Elliot Phoenix was a hired gun for a major recording artist that had been around for over fifty years. Just last night she'd posted a video clip jamming next to a god of rock and roll. Not like he was stalking. Top music vloggers loved interviewing her. She even had her own signature guitar line. Elliot Phoenix was the hottest, most musically sound guitarist in the industry. It surprised him that she hadn't been hired permanently by a band or artist.

The lights went out and shortly returned to red neon lights resembling fire. Smoke filled the stage, and even where he stood, he could feel the crowd's anticipation of the return of The Phoenix. Through the smoke, she emerged, shredding the riff of Ozzy Osborne's "Miracle Man." Dressed in black ripped jeans, a black rock concert T-shirt cut into a tank top, and black boots, she looked like a phoenix rising from the ashes. *Fucking beautiful!*

"Jake Quin." Someone addressed him from behind, breaking the spell he'd been under.

He turned around to find Dylan Grace, lead singer of Gracefall, walking toward him, filling the room with rock-and-roll swagger. "Bro, you made it." Dylan shook his hand firmly, followed by a welcoming bro hug. "When did you get in?"

Jake looked at his watch. "Three hours ago," he yelled over the music.

Dylan pulled down his aviators, his eyes bloodshot and pupils dilated. Being an ex-cop, Jake recognized the rocker's cocaine eyes. "Tell me you left that fringe jacket at home."

Jake snickered. "Actually, since it made such a lasting impression, I thought I'd wear it at the first show."

Dylan laughed as he put his arm around Jake, leading them to a row of red semicircular leather booths lining the wall. "You're going to fit in just fine, dude."

Jake picked the side of the booth where he could see the band and slid in. Dylan sat across from him, lounging back in the seat. His aviators were back on. "So, are you ready for this wild trip?"

Inside, Jake was busting at the seams with excitement. Hell yeah, he was ready for this. He couldn't wait to share the stage with Gracefall and show the world what he was made of. Musically, he had so much to offer and looked forward to working with the guys. Jake cooled his shit, taking in a deep breath. "As much as I can be."

"You've never been in a band before, have you?"

"In college."

"Oh nice, a college grad."

"More like college dropout." Jake shrugged.

"Now, that's more rock and roll." Dylan chugged from the half-full Jack Daniels bottle that had been sitting on the table. "So, tell me, Jake, what is it that you want to get out of this deal? Fortune and fame? Chicks? We have the hottest groupies."

That was a loaded question. Was Dylan testing him or just making small talk to feel him out? After his epic jacket fail, Jake didn't want to say the wrong thing and ruin his opportunity with the band, yet he wanted to be honest. "Well, it's definitely not chicks."

Seemingly surprised by his response, Dylan leaned in and whispered, "Are you gay?"

What?

Dylan downplayed his initial reaction. "I mean, it's cool if you are."

"No." Jake shook his head. "I'm not gay. When it comes to women, I'm unlucky."

"Really? Do tell." Dylan eagerly waited for his story.

Jake exhaled heavily, thinking about how much detail to reveal from his Vegas wedding. Did he start with the runaway bride or the fact he was still married to a ghost? "So, about a year ago me and my girlfriend ran off to Vegas to get married."

"Jailhouse Rock Elvis or the rhinestone eagle jumpsuit Elvis?"

"Eagle jumpsuit."

"Fuck yeah, dude!" Dylan threw him metal horns.

"Yeah, well, I woke up the next morning hungover, and my wife was gone."

"Bro!"

"Yep, she left a note basically telling me that the whole night was a mistake."

"She divorced your ass before the honeymoon was over, huh?"

Feeling uncomfortable, Jake rubbed the back of his neck. "Not quite. Technically we're still married."

"So, she came back?"

"No, still taking time to reflect." Jake used hand quotes to emphasize the word reflect.

"Okay. So, you're still married to the woman who left your ass after the wedding?"

Yep, he'd buried that skeleton deep in the ground. "Back to the question. What I want out of this deal is to create music with technically sound musicians. It's that simple."

Dylan leaned back, resuming his relaxed swagger attitude. "It's not all that simple, Jake. This business isn't for everyone. It takes an insane amount of hard work to get to the top, and once you're there, it takes even more work to stay there. When Gracefall performs, it's our time to prove to the world that we belong and give it our all. I wish I could say everything else is bullshit, but it's not. Everyone wants a piece of you. Groupies want to fuck you. Managers want their cut of everything. The pressure to write new material is mentally straining when you can't even process what day it is. The whole thing is like a huge machine that's constantly needing to be fed blood, sweat, and tears." Dylan shoved his hands through his hair. "I'm sorry, dude, to be a buzz kill."

Jake saw the effects rock and roll had on Dylan, from the cocaine eyes to drowning in a bottle of Jack, but something was telling him it wasn't all rock and roll that had left its mark on Dylan. There was something deeper here—the rocker was lost. "I'm sure it's not easy, and I know I have a lot to learn, but I'm willing to do whatever it takes. Gracefall is my family now, and making music will always be my priority."

"Good, because I like you, and I don't like too many people." Dylan took another sip from the bottle. "Welcome to the family."

Jake nodded, then realized that if this night got more intense, he'd need a drink. "I'm going to the bar."

"Good call. Everyone should be here soon. We're meeting in the back room."

"I'll be there." Jake slid out of the booth and headed to the bar as he processed everything, from seeing his rocker crush Elliot Phoenix on stage to having a heart-to-heart with Dylan Grace. Was he genuinely ready for this?

He'd never toured before, so life on the road would be a challenge. Would the fans accept him as Moxley's replacement? Probably not. Jake would have to prove himself worthy. He was confident in his playing that he would. Then there was the dynamics of the band; where did he fit in? How was the band going to handle the new guy living in the shadow of Moxley Sims? How was Jake going to handle it?

Jake reached the bar and ordered a drink, his mind still on overdrive. Was he getting cold feet about joining Gracefall? Overall, his biggest fear was being musically silenced. There was an ideology in rock bands that new members had to pay their dues before contributing musically. Jake was already a proven studio musician, but he had no street cred.

He had the heart and determination to fulfill his dream. Besides, going back to the Tin Flask so his brother could tell him "told you so" wasn't an option. He wasn't fucking this up. After a few drinks, his nerves would settle. He was balls-to-the-wall in.

Jake sat at the bar, sipping his drink for a while, lost in thought when someone sat next to him and ordered a drink. Nonchalantly, he glanced over to see it was a woman with long bleach-blonde hair and dark roots wearing a black leather jacket. She pinned him with her catlike blue eyes and flashed a big smile. "Hi."

Jake's breath hitched in his throat. *Holy shit! Elliot Phoenix! Say something, asshole!*

"Hey." He played it cool, trying not to lose his shit. "Kickass show tonight." *Really kickass.*

She giggled and looked him up and down. "Thanks."

"I must have missed the announcement about you joining the Crazy Bitches."

"So, you follow me on social media?"

"Yeah, I like to check you out—I mean, I read your posts about guitars." God, his nerves were rattled.

"Right." She smiled and took a drink of water from the

glass the bartender had placed in front of her. "So, what's your name, Creepy Pete?"

"Jake Quin, and I'm not a creepy stalker."

"I know." She bumped his shoulder with hers playfully. "I'm joking. Lighten up."

He smiled, feeling slightly embarrassed. "It's really cool that you have a tribute band for Ozzy."

"Oh, that's not my band. I was filling in for their guitarist for the night. I'm good friends with OzHerrella, the lead vocalist."

"OzHerrella?"

"Yeah, she's the Crazy Bitches' Princess of Darkness."

"Oh, got it."

"So, who are you, Jake?" She flashed him another beautiful smile that he was really getting used to. "They don't just let anyone up here to mingle."

"I'm a studio musician. I've played lead and/or rhythm guitar on numerous heavy metal and hard rock albums."

"Really?" She studied him for a second. "You don't look like a rocker."

"What's that supposed to mean?"

"No tattoos. You don't wear leather. Your hair isn't long enough."

Ouch, he thought his shoulder-length dark shaggy locks were on point tonight.

She shrugged as she reached for her glass. "You're too pretty for rock and roll." She took a sip.

"Huh." Was that an insult or compliment? He was above-average height for a man and still had his fit cop bod. Women at the bar were always complementing him on his blue eyes and his boy-next-door look. Hell, he even had a goatee he kept trimmed short because chicks liked it. Stacy had. He rubbed his chin.

She gave him the side-eye. "It's a good thing." And there was that infectious smile again.

"I'm here tonight to sign with Gracefall. I'm their new lead guitarist." He shouldn't have said anything, but he was feeling inadequate compared to Elliot. This was his opportunity to impress the insanely sexy guitar goddess.

Her smile faded. "Is that so?"

"Yeah, I'm meeting the guys in just a few minutes to go over the details." Jake still felt like he was living someone else's dream. By the end of the night, he'd be part of Gracefall.

"Well, Jake." She stood and acted as if he'd said something wrong. Did rockers turn her off? Because up to this point, he was feeling good about the flirting going on between them. "Good luck."

He couldn't let the night end without asking her out. "Hey, maybe after my meeting we could hook up and talk some more." *Shit!* He sounded too desperate.

"I can't. I'm busy."

Inside, Jake deflated like a balloon. He turned back to the bar. "That's cool. It was nice talking to you." He waived to the bartender for another drink.

First, he smelled her sweet perfume. Then, he felt her lips brush against his earlobe. "Don't worry, Pretty Boy, you'll be seeing me soon."

hat the hell was going on? Elliot found a quiet spot on the upper level of The Black Veil, which was easier to do than on the lower level. All the rockers and their entourage hung out here to either catch a show or just be seen, but tonight, she'd been there for business. It had been almost a week since she'd auditioned for Gracefall's lead guitar position. Three days later, her manager, Jill, had called saying that the guys had chosen her. In fact, she was here tonight to sign the contract. So, what was Jake talking about? Had Jill lied?

Elliot pulled out her cell and texted Jill, who was late.

Elliot: Where are you!!!

Jill: I just checked into the hotel. I'll be there in fifteen. What's wrong?

Elliot: Just get here!

Elliot pocketed her phone and took in a long breath, trying to keep her shit together. Her life depended on this gig. She couldn't lose it to a studio musician pretty boy.

It had been no coincidence that she'd filled in for the guitarist of Crazy Bitches the same night she was here to meet with Gracefall. It was a strategic move to give the guys one more taste of what she was made of. There would be no doubt she was the one.

Because she was a girl in a male-dominated world, she had to work harder to prove that she wasn't some hot chick behind a guitar. She could actually play. She loved to watch the boys' mouths drop when she plugged in and dazzled them with her guitar skills.

Now, she had no idea what was going on.

It was a long fifteen minutes, but Jill finally arrived and looked as if she'd run a 5K. She was catching her breath as she readjusted her form-fitting black suit jacket and matching skirt. Her leather briefcase was in her other hand. "Fucking Sunset," she huffed, fixing a loose tendril of blonde hair that had fallen from the bun on top of her head.

Jill Mason was a powerhouse in the industry and had been Elliot's business manager since the beginning of her career. She didn't quit until her clients' goals and visions were met. Because of Jill's connections, Elliot had shared the stage with a diverse range of musicians, for which she was grateful.

But after five years of bouncing around from band to band and not knowing when she'd be hired again to fill a spot, she wanted something more secure. Not only for herself but for her five-year-old son. "We got a problem."

"What do you mean?" Jill had herself back together and was ready to kick some ass.

"After the show, I met a guy at the bar—"

"Doesn't sound like a problem to me."

"He said he was here tonight to sign a contract with Gracefall. He said he was their new lead guitarist."

Elliot watched Jill's cheeks turn red. "Are you serious? What's his name?"

"Jake Quin."

"Ellie, don't worry about a thing. No one is going pull this shit on you. Fucking rock stars." Jill took out her phone from her briefcase. "I'm Googling him now. I want to go in knowing who I'm dealing with. I've already been warned about their band manager, Davidson. I hear he's a real piece of work."

"Jake said he was a studio musician." Elliot folded her arms against her chest and began to pace in front of Jill. "I can't lose this gig, Jill."

Her manager looked up from her phone in awe. "Oh, wow!"

Elliot stopped pacing and looked over Jill's shoulder at her phone. "What? Is it bad?"

"Um, he's hot."

Elliot rolled her eyes. "Seriously? I don't care how fuckable Jake Quin is. He's the enemy right now."

"Sorry. He just caught me off guard." Jill continued to read his internet bio. "His creds are impressive. He's worked with many popular artists. I can see why Gracefall wants him."

This didn't help her situation at all.

"Listen, Ellie." Jill shoved her phone back into the briefcase. "You have nothing to worry about. I know how much you want this for Elijah."

More than anything she wanted to spend more time with her son. Being a permanent member of Gracefall would give them stability. She wouldn't have to leave him with her sister, Sarah, while she was on tour like she did now. She wouldn't have to keep her son a secret anymore. They could travel the world together.

Jill straightened. "Here's the plan. We'll go in and listen to what they have to offer. This could all be a misunderstanding. Don't say anything. Let me do all talking. And whatever you do, don't bring up Elijah. I don't want them using him or anything else against you."

Elliot had done everything to keep her son out of the limelight. Not even the paparazzi knew about him. It was really a shame she had to be so secretive, but she'd been scared that no one would hire her if they knew she had a son.

It had been bad enough that her nightmarish marriage and ugly divorce to Dax Gage, lead singer for the heavy metal band Death Tribute, had been smeared all over social media and television. It was right after the divorce that she'd found out she was pregnant. The snake had left her with nothing. Thank God for Sarah taking her in and picking up the broken pieces.

Elliot had taken a year off to get her life back, have Eli, and reinvent her career. That's when she'd hired Jill to be her manager. It had taken five years to build up her brand and finally make a name for herself. She owed it all to Jill.

Up until this point, Elliot had been a hired gun. She'd been hired to be the lead guitarist for top solo artists who needed a band for a tour. To keep a job, she had to be dependable, and let's face it, being a single mom didn't look reliable on a rock-and-roll resume. With her ex-husband out of the family panorama, she was the sole provider. She had to do whatever it took to keep money coming in, so Jill and Elliot had decided for Eli's wellbeing and for her career that it was best that no one knew about him.

Elliot was so close to finally having a permanent gig and being able to bring Eli on the road with her. She'd already researched tutors so he wouldn't miss his first year of school. "I'm tired of the lie, Jill, but I understand."

"You know it's hard being a woman in this business. I'm sorry, but we must play the game if you want in this band."

"I know."

"Then let's go in there and kick some ass." Jill smiled. God, she loved this woman's confidence.

Elliot followed Jill into the meeting room, trying to look as confident as her manager. From the outside, she pulled it off, but from the inside, she was a nervous wreck. She needed this gig.

Joe Grace, the drummer of Gracefall, stood and shook her hand. "It's good seeing you again."

She smiled and shook his hand. "Likewise."

"So, you remember Dylan and Tyler."

She nodded and glanced over at the guys. Dylan asserted his typical lead singer swagger, leaning back in his chair with his arms folded and his legs stretched out. His feet were crossed at the ankles, and he slid his aviators down his nose. "The fucking Phoenix has graced us with her presence." He clapped his hands slowly.

Before she could take offense to his remarks, Tyler stood and shook her hand. "Don't mind him. He's cranky."

Dylan pushed his shades back over her eyes. "Whatever, dude."

"Anyway," Joe continued as he stood next to a gorgeous blonde who looked vaguely familiar. "I believe you met my fiancée, Melody Sterling, at the audition."

Right, that's where she'd met her. She was the daughter of the legendary drummer Leo Sterling.

"Nice to meet you again, Elliot. Awesome show tonight."

"Thanks."

Joe continued with the introductions. "The badass chick with the pink hair is Cherry Lane. She's our new tour manager."

"I can't believe I'm meeting the Queen of Shred." Cherry shook her hand. "It's an honor."

"It's an honor to be here."

"This here is Davidson." Joe motioned to the chic and sleek big guy sitting at the head of the conference table. He looked as if he'd stepped right out of a men's fashion magazine with his short, slicked-back fad hairstyle. "He's our manager. He'll be speaking on our behalf."

Davidson nodded, and his eyes never stopped reading the stack of papers sitting in front of him. Elliot shrugged it off. She had Jill on her side, and once she let her do her thing, they wouldn't know what had hit them.

Elliot turned to the only guy in the room who hadn't been introduced yet, Jake Quin. He looked as confused as she felt.

All eyes were on Jill, waiting for Elliot to make introductions. "Everyone, this is Jill Mason, my manager. She'll be speaking on my behalf."

Davidson's gaze shot up from the documents, and he looked Jill up and down as if he'd seen a golden Greek goddess. Elliot wasn't surprised by his reaction. Jill's beauty was part of her powerhouse image.

"Nice to meet you, Davidson." Jill held out her hand, nails freshly manicured. Davidson had the same reaction that most men had when meeting her for the first time. Mouth wide open, jaw to the floor, lust-filled eyes... she'd seen it all before.

Davidson took a minute to process the beauty in front of him. Finally, he shook her hand. "The pleasure is all mine, Miss Mason."

Elliot sat down and allowed Jill to reel him in and work her magic before she went in for the kill. She hated playing games. It reminded her of how her ex-husband would manipulate her. With him, there were always strings attached.

"Do these drugs with me, and I'll give you mind-blowing sex."

"If you love me, you'll do it."

As the lead singer of his band, everyone in Dax's entourage loved him. His fans worshiped him. And when Elliot got invited to go on tour with him, it was an opportunity she couldn't turn down. Musically, she'd admired Dax Gage. And to say she wasn't smitten with Dax right from the start would be a lie.

Elliot had gone into the relationship living the rock star dream. Too bad for Dax that his life's motto was live fast, die young. She went along for the ride and crashed and burned until she knew she had to leave the sex, drugs, and rock-and-roll chaos.

Beyond the partying, the head games were exhausting. He'd manipulated her, knowing her weakness was pleasing him. Never again did she allow someone to have that much power over her. She'd left Dax, not knowing she had been pregnant. But not even a pregnancy would sober Dax up. It was sad that a father wanted nothing to do with his son, but she wasn't pushing the issue. Eli needed a positive male influence in his life, and since she wasn't looking for a relationship anytime soon, she'd taken on both mother and father responsibilities.

It had taken Elliot five years to get her life back. She was still a work in progress, but she was on the right road.

No, Elliot wanted straightforward conversation. No lies. She'd leave the negotiation games for Jill.

Everyone sat down. Davidson handed Jake and Jill a set of papers. He cleared his throat as he began. "This is an unusual situation we have found ourselves in. We can't choose between the two of you." He glanced at Jake then at

Elliot. "So, Gracefall and I have come up with a solution that I think will benefit everyone. As you know, replacing a member of a band changes the dynamics of a band. Then there's finding the right chemistry. I think you can see where I'm going."

Jill crossed her legs and set the contract on the table. "Actually, Mr.—"

"Just Davidson."

"Davidson. Where are you going with this? I was under the impression that Elliot was to be Gracefall's new lead guitarist. The only deal I see being made here is for my client."

"I apologize for any misunderstandings, but nowhere has it been stated that either one solely has the gig."

"Well, this is very deceiving."

"Just hear me out. I think this deal will benefit us both."

Jill folded her arms on top of the table, turning on bitch mode. "I'm all ears."

"I want to hire Elliot and Jake to tour with Gracefall in our upcoming U.S. tour for six months. Like a trial period. Then we'll choose who will best fit the band."

"Are you joking? You're telling me that you want Elliot Phoenix to audition for Gracefall for the next six months with hopes she'll be hired."

"Yes."

Jill looked at Elliot and shook her head. "I've never heard of this before."

Elliot couldn't believe what she was hearing. Did they actually want her to give up the next six months of her life in hopes she'll get the gig? No way. She didn't want to be a hired gun.

"You do understand you're asking Elliot to put her career

on hold for six months. She'd be better off starting a solo career."

"Well, Ms. Mason. If you turn to page ten in the contract, you'll see there are generous compensation benefits. I'll read a few. A five-hundred-thousand-dollar signing bonus. We want both Jake and Elliot to know we are invested in them and their careers. A tour bus equipped with everything they'll need to learn the song lineup. However, the bus will be shared between both Jake and Elliot. Let's see." He skimmed the rest. "Paid promo. Hair and makeup stylist." He looked up from the contract. "I mean, everything you'll need is right here. I do recommend that you have a music lawyer to review royalties."

"We receive royalties for the six months we're on tour?" Jake asked.

"Yes."

"Sweet." Jake went back to reviewing the contract.

Elliot's mouth dropped. She didn't get this kind of treatment as a hired gun. Yeah, there had been some excellent benefits, but not like this. The signing bonus alone was extremely generous.

"Of course, once we choose one of you, there will be a renegotiation of the contract."

"I'm not sure I like this deal," Jill said, playing hardball. "This sounds like a spin on American Idol and Survivor. Survive six months with Gracefall and win a spot in the band."

"Jill," Elliot whispered, trying not to call her out. "We should talk about this."

Dylan sat up and turned to Davidson. "Putting it that way, I'm not sure I like this idea. Sounds cheesy to me."

"Well, Ms. Phoenix." Davidson looked at Elliot. "It's still Miss, right?"

She ignored the low blow and nodded.

"If it's a no-deal, then Jake can take the gig. It would sure make my life easier and save Clef Tonic Records a buttload of money."

"Wait a second," Elliot interrupted. "This is the first time I'm hearing about this deal after I was under the impression you wanted me to be the lead guitarist. When do you need to know?"

"Twenty-four hours."

Elliot looked at Jill in question. Twenty-four hours didn't seem long enough.

Jill nodded, reassuring Elliot that everything was fine. "Okay then, you'll be hearing from me in twenty-four hours."

"How about you, Jake?" Davidson asked.

"I have my attorney on speed dial. Not a problem."

"Good." Davidson shoved his copy of the contract in his briefcase. "We're done here."

"About fucking time." Joe stood, and Melody followed his lead. "If you need me, I'll be busy." He wiggled his brows at Melody and smacked her ass.

"Joe!" Melody playfully slapped his chest. She looked over at Elliot and Jake. "I'm sorry. It's way past his bedtime. It was nice meeting you both. Hope to see you guys on tour."

Elliot smiled. "Me too."

Davidson rested his arms on the table, leaning toward Jill. "How about I buy you a drink?"

"Are you serious!" Dylan shot up from the chair. "Ash doesn't deserve this, asshole." He stormed out of the room.

Davidson shrugged.

"Who's Ash?" Jill asked.

"My girlfriend." He smirked.

"I'll keep that in mind." Jill stood and grabbed her briefcase. "One drink. I'll be at the bar."

The room emptied, leaving Elliot alone with Jake. As she watched him, she realized the once intriguing hot rocker that had been sitting at the bar moments ago was now the enemy, which was too bad because he'd seemed like a nice guy.

Jake broke the silence. "This is a shock to me, too."

Elliot put her guard up. Nothing was going to keep her from getting this gig, no matter how much Jake tried to charm her. And he would, just to get what he wanted. Rockers were all the same, and she wasn't falling for that trick ever again. She crossed her arms. "So, what are we going to do about it? I mean, I'm the right choice."

"Are you suggesting I drop out and give the gig to you? I would have thought Elliot Phoenix liked a little competition."

"No, that's not what I'm suggesting. I have no doubt who's the better guitarist, and it will be my pleasure knocking your dick in the ground, Pretty Boy."

"Have you ever heard me play?" Jake pinned her with bright blue eyes that somehow left her breathless. "I didn't think so." Jake placed his hands on his hips. "I've heard you play. Hell, I've idolized you."

"Don't try to be my friend, Jake. Flattery will get you nowhere."

"Trust me, I know where I stand."

"Good. Then you know you're the enemy, and I will not surrender. This gig is mine."

Jake shrugged. "We'll see."

He left the room, and finally, she could breathe again. Jake was dangerous in more ways than one. When she'd seen him sitting at the bar, he'd looked different from the typical rocker she was used to seeing at nightclubs, so she had to meet him. If things had been different, she wouldn't have minded meeting him for a drink and getting to know him. He was cute, like the boy next door. But now, no way. He was a rocker, and she'd already been there, done that.

4

*J*ake's cellphone rang, jerking him awake. Half asleep and hungover, he fumbled around the side table, searching for his phone. Staying at the club with Dylan had turned into a night of heavy drinking and hanging out with a few members of Whiplash. As he picked up his phone, the room spun.

"Jake," he answered in a deep, raspy voice.

"Hi, Jake. It's Kimmy Anderson, the public relations representative for Gracefall." Her chipper voice went straight through his head.

"Hi," he grumbled.

"Davidson wanted me to set up a meeting with you to go over some promotional things. Are you available, say, in thirty minutes?"

Before he could process anything, Kimmy answered for him.

"Good. I'll come to you. Meet me in the hotel lobby lounge." She hung up, leaving Jake in the wake of her storm.

Jake dropped his phone onto the bed. He rubbed his eyes, trying to remember how he'd made it back to his hotel suite. He remembered shooting the shit with Dylan and Tyler over several rounds of Jack Daniels at The Veil. He recalled sending over the contract to his lawyer to review late last night. Or had it been early this morning?

And he definitely remembered meeting Elliot Phoenix. She was beautiful, and he'd felt a connection until the bomb was dropped. He didn't want to be her enemy for the next six months. He just wanted things to be cool between them since they'd be sharing a bus. That is if she signed her contract, which he hoped she did. Beating Elliot Phoenix for the Gracefall position would look good on his rocker creds.

Jake sat up in bed. His head throbbed, and his stomach turned. *Fuck!* He prayed he'd feel better after a shower; however, he'd be feeling the effects of last night long into the day with the amount of liquor in his system.

He pried himself off the bed and went into the bathroom, turning on the shower. Then he ditched yesterday's clothes and stepped inside. The warm spray slid down his body, awakening him. In his younger days, he would have been able to recover quicker. Now in his thirties, yeah, recovering took a bit longer.

After a quick shower and changing into some fresh clothes, Jake made his way downstairs to the lobby lounge with a bottle of water in tow. As he entered the lounge, he saw Elliot sitting at a table drinking a cup of coffee as she scrolled through her phone. What was she doing here?

Jake walked over to her table, knowing damn well it would piss her off. He was the enemy. "Hey." He pulled out the chair across from her and sat down before she could protest.

"Make yourself at home much?" Her eyes never left her phone.

"So, are you staying here at the hotel or just here to meet Kimmy?"

"Yes, and yes. Why do you ask?"

He shrugged. "I don't know. I thought maybe you lived in Cali with all the other rock stars."

She set her phone down. "I live in Nevada."

"No shit. Me too. Reno."

"Carson City."

"Small world."

And there it was. He got a smile. The same beautiful smile he'd seen at the bar last night. He locked eyes with her and stayed there, taking her in a little bit longer than he should have. Her bleach-blonde hair was pulled back into a ponytail. Her eyes weren't lined in black eyeliner like they had been the last time he'd seen her. She looked comfortable and casual in her rock concert tank top and jeans. He looked away, retreating from the spell he'd been under.

"So." Jake leaned in, resting his arms on the table. "I'm guessing since you're here waiting for Kimmy, you've signed the contract."

"I'm all in, Pretty Boy. Hope you're ready." Her lips cocked into a sideways smile, drawing his attention to her mouth. "How about you?"

"Signed it last night."

"Is that why you look like what the cat dragged in?"

"Ouch." Jake acted offended, but he wasn't. He actually liked her bantering. "Yeah, stayed out drinking with the guys to celebrate." He ran his hand through his damp hair, pushing it back off his forehead. "Not sure how I got back to my room."

"Typical rocker bullshit." Elliot turned back to her phone, seemingly not interested in the conversation.

"And what's a typical rocker, Elliot, because last night you said I was, and I quote, "Too pretty for rock and roll.""

She leaned in and narrowed her gaze at him. "Maybe I had you all wrong." She looked him up and down. "Maybe you do like wild parties and wilder women. What's your drug of choice? Pot, coke, alcohol?"

He leaned back and took a long sip from his bottle of water. As much as he wanted to prove Elliot wrong, he decided not to give her anything she could use against him. Especially him being an ex-cop. "Think what you want."

She crossed her arms over her chest, which pushed her breasts to the top of her tank top. Jake swallowed hard as he fought the urge to look. "I think I'll keep my first impression of you, Pretty Boy. Rockers can hold their liquor. In fact, I knew a guy who drank until his pancreas exploded."

"Seriously?"

"Yep, toured with him for a year. Ten bottles of wine a day, and that was him trying to cut back."

"Wow. Can't say I've worked under those conditions. Typically, I lay down my guitar tracks, play with the band, and leave."

"You've never toured before?"

"Nope."

"Pretty Boy, you've got a lot to learn."

"Maybe you can teach me."

She glared at him, making him regret what he'd just said. What was he thinking? He was the enemy.

"Hi, guys." Jake turned to see Kimmy standing next to him. Thank God. She'd just saved him from making a bigger fool out of himself.

"So, listen, we don't have much time." Kimmy sat down. "I have a photographer lined up today for some promo shots. Davidson's marketing plan is to play on a friendly feud between you two. You know, something playful. Elliot, we don't really want you to kick Jake's ass," Kimmy joked.

"That's no fun," Elliot said as she glared at Jake.

"But there's no feud between us," Jake said.

"I know, but you'll play one on TV." Kimmy winked. "I have a car waiting for us outside. We should get a move on. LA traffic is a bitch."

"That's okay." Elliot took out her phone. "Jill can drive me."

"Oh, no need." Kimmy waved Elliot off as she stood. "There's plenty of room in the Suburban."

Jake leaned in. "What's wrong, Elliot? I'll share the backseat with you. I won't bite." He smirked.

Elliot surrendered. She gathered her things and stood, all the while glaring at Jake. God, he really loved getting under her skin.

*a*s soon as Jake and Elliot got to the photo studio inside the industrial-style, urban-chic home of Andrew Black, who, according to Kimmy, was THE photographer of the rock stars, they were whisked off to makeup and wardrobe.

Before Jake knew what was happening, his ass was plopped down in front of a mirror framed in blinding lights with a dude behind him wrapping his hair in foil. *What the fuck?*

"Oh, don't worry. It's only for texture."

Jake looked at the guy in the mirror and checked out his shaggy black hair and blond highlights. "Wait a second." Jake sat up. "I'm a rocker, not a dude in a boy band."

Kimmy rushed in with a rolling rack of clothes. "Don't worry, Jake, you're in good hands with Marco. Trust me."

Jake looked back into the mirror where Marco was giving him a "told you so" smirk.

Fuck!

"Relax, Jake." Marco eased him back into the chair. "I got you."

In a whirlwind of aluminum foil and hair dye solution, Marco had Jake's brain completely protected from government mind probing and alien overlords in no time at all.

Marco left, saying he'd return in ten to check on him. Before Jake could respond, Marco bounced out of the cubicle and into the one next door. He heard Elliot's voice and a round of laughter and "oh my god, yes" as they discussed her hair. Jake cracked a smile. Elliot didn't have to try hard to look hot. She'd make bald look sexy.

He just wished he could read her. One minute she was flirty, the next cold-blooded. The next six months would be a lot easier if at least they could get along. Yeah, he got it— he was the enemy. But it didn't need to be that way. He was here to win fair and square.

The vibe he got was that she didn't trust him. He understood that. She didn't know him, but how could he prove to her that she could trust him if she shut him out? Then again, why should he care?

It wasn't as if he had any plans to make a move on Elliot. She was out of his league. She was gorgeous with her catlike blue eyes and high cheekbones, and she had a confidence about her like she could take on the world. He admired that. For him, he was used to doing what people expected of him. But not now. He was living his dream for the next six months with no regrets. Elliot Phoenix would only distract him, and that wasn't going to happen.

After a quick rinse, cut, and blow-dry, Kimmy had Jake dressed in a short-sleeved black denim shirt and black jeans, which looked like they had been bedazzled by a metalhead fan. They had chains, silver spikes, studded front pockets, and leather lace-ups on the thighs. Jake looked in the mirror. He had to hand it to Kimmy; new hair style and all, he looked like a rock star.

"Oh good, you're dressed." Kimmy rushed in with chain and leather necklaces hanging from her arm. "I wasn't sure if you were a dog tag or Celtic cross kind of guy, so I brought both."

He turned to Kimmy, and by her expression, she wasn't happy. "What?"

She set the jewelry down on the table and walked toward him. "You've got to lose the first five buttons." She unbuttoned his shirt, then took a step back. "Much better." She returned to the table, examining the jewelry.

"Is this all necessary?" He was beginning to feel like a fake.

"Image is everything." She returned with a Celtic cross hanging from a strap of leather, then put it on him. "You want to look as if you fit the band's image." She put a black wristband on his right wrist. "The clothes make you feel like a rocker, right?"

Jake looked in the mirror. "The jeans are kinda badass."

Kimmy stood behind him and fluffed his hair as she looked at him through the mirror. "You are one hot rocker, my friend. Chicks are going to go crazy when they finally see you on stage."

"Kimmy, I'm not looking to fuck a bunch of chicks. I just want to play music."

"Right." She nodded. "That's what they all say."

Jake shook his head. "I'm serious."

"Okay, rock star, whatever you say." She walked toward the door. "Follow me. Dylan, Joe, and Tyler are waiting for you in the living room. You can stay there until it's your turn in front of the lens."

He followed her down the hall.

"Davidson wants individual shots, as well as some with

you and Elliot together. We'll use these images for social media, the website, all sorts of good stuff, so it's crucial to nail this shoot, okay?"

"Nothing like bringing on the pressure, Kimmy."

"If you need to loosen up, there's whiskey on the table. I don't want to know what else is out there." She turned around and tapped her nose.

Jake walked into the living room, where the guys were making themselves at home. Joe was on the couch, texting, Dylan was pouring himself a drink from the minbar, and Tyler was checking out the photoshoot setup behind a wall of glass that separated the living room from the studio.

"Hey, hey, hey," Dylan greeted him. "Want a drink?"

"I'm good." The thought of alcohol turned his stomach.

"Bro, I totally expected to see you in a fringe leather jacket," Dylan joked.

"You're going to keep busting my balls for that one, aren't you?"

Dylan gave Jake a bro hug. "Fuck yeah, dude."

Joe got up from the couch and stretched. "So, have you met Andrew yet?"

"No."

"Dude, you haven't met him?" Dylan exclaimed.

"It's been crazy. Makeup, wardrobe—I haven't had time to breathe."

Dylan looked down at Jake's pants. "I was going to say I love those fucking pants."

"Badass." Jake did a half-turn, showing the metal attire off.

Joe shook his head. "Okay, fashionistas, let's focus here."

Dylan rolled his eyes. "You'd think that having a smoking-hot fiancée would put him in a good mood."

Joe shrugged off Dylan's comment. "Andrew can be a bit moody."

"Oh, that's rich," Dylan interrupted.

Joe glared at his brother. "Fuck off." He returned to Jake and placed his hand on his shoulder. "It's best if you don't talk and just do what he says, or else there will be drama."

"I'll keep that in mind," Jake replied.

"Holy shit!" Tyler looked through the glass wall into the studio. "You've got to see this."

Jake, Dylan, and Joe joined Tyler as they watched Elliot walk into the studio from a side door. Jake's eyes went straight to her tits. He couldn't help it. The black lace camisole looked more like lingerie, which had him thinking about silk sheets and two hot bodies tangled together. He checked her out down to the black leather pants that looked like they had been painted on. Holy fuck, how was he supposed to stand next to her and keep his dick in check?

There was an oversized mahogany leather chair in the middle of a red satin backdrop. Jake watched her talk to the photographer, then walk over to the chair and lie across it. Andrew placed the guitar so the neck of the instrument was resting between her tits. Then he positioned her legs so they were slightly bent, resting on the arm of the chair and showing off her red stilettos. Andrew took a step back, observing his creation. "Now fuck me with those eyes." He broke out the camera and began clicking away.

Jake stood, watching Elliot. This softer, sexier side of her was entirely different from the badass rock chick on stage, and he liked it.

"Fuck," Joe exhaled. "I told you this wasn't a good idea."

Tyler looked at Jake. "Dude, you're sharing a bus with her?"

Dylan handed Jake his drink. "You're so fucked, dude."

~

*E*lliot knew exactly what she was doing as she posed with her guitar, killing her photoshoot. She had an audience, which helped her turned up the heat. Yeah, it didn't bother her showing off her assets and using them to her advantage if it meant getting that much closer to her goal. Call it job security.

Andrew put his camera down and motioned for Jake to come into the studio. As Jake walked in, her breath hitched in her chest. His black denim shirt was form-fitting, showing off just enough of his toned biceps to catch her eye. His eyes were bluer. It must be the hint of black eyeliner bringing them out. He looked like a sexy rock star, but of course, he wasn't. She shook her head, breaking free from even the slightest thought that Jake was hot.

She stood with her hands resting on the head of her guitar as Andrew informed Jake what to do. "We're going to start off with some competitive shots like a guitar war." Andrew's assistant handed Jake a guitar.

"Guitar war?" Jake questioned.

"Yes." He moved Jake toward Elliot. "Just act like you're going to hit each with your guitars."

Elliot eyed Jake as he joined her in front of the leather chair.

"So, we're supposed to act like we don't like each other?" Jake asked.

"Not a problem for me, Pretty Boy." Elliot smirked.

"Yeah, I thought as much." Jake took the guitar and held it like a baseball bat. "Let's do this, slugger."

Elliot rolled her eyes. He had a way of making the stupidest things sound funny. She stood in front of him and swung her guitar over her shoulder. With the other hand, she made a fist at him and growled.

"Yes!" She heard Andrew cheer. "I want more."

Back and forth, they continued to battle it out.

She had to admit, this photoshoot was turning out to be fun. And it hadn't hurt that Jake's new rock-and-roll look was hot.

He's the enemy.

"Okay." Andrew paused and checked the shots on his camera. "I'd like to get a couple shots of you two together. Give something sexy."

Elliot's smile slid off her face. *What?* She glanced at Jake, and her heart thundered in her chest. *Sexy?*

Jake slowly walked behind her and put his hands around her waist, pulling her close. Fuck, he smelled so good. The scent reminded her of bourbon and orange blossoms. He looked down at her, and his smoldering blue stare created a heatwave within her. He was only an inch taller than her, but she felt petite next to him for some reason. Elliot swallowed hard as his hand slid across her stomach. She let her guard down and leaned her back against him, taking in his body heat.

His lips brushed against her earlobe. "Are you okay?"

A shiver streaked down her spine. Oh, she was more than okay. She couldn't remember the last time she allowed someone to touch her this way, but the feeling of being on cloud nine was still there. It was scary how easily she'd let her guard down. Yeah, Jake's touch felt good, but it was just a feeling, nothing more. "I'm good," she whispered back.

"It will be over soon. Then you can go back hating me." The sarcasm in his voice cut a little. At least he knew where he stood. And it was a good reminder to keep that separation.

"Not soon enough." The wall guarding her heart and her career was up again and would stay up. Eli deserved a better life. She wanted a better life, and this job would get that for her and her son.

6

One week later, Elliot was on a private jet heading back to California to catch Gracefall's tour bus. It hadn't been nearly enough time to pack and say goodbye to Elijah, Sarah, and her mother, Janet, for the next six months, but she'd made do. Elliot held a faded and worn picture of her and Eli in her hands. She pressed it against her heart. This gig had to happen. Elliot couldn't bear another tour without her son with her. She was missing precious moments, like his first day of school.

Her mind wandered to Jake. Who was he leaving behind? A girlfriend? A wife? Kids? And why did she care?

Elliot dropped her gaze out the oval window. She was ready to start the tour and kick Jake's ass. Pretty Boy had never experienced life on the road. It would either break him or make him. Chances are, he wouldn't last. It took dedication and drive to be a musician on the road. Elliot had both, and she would survive. She couldn't wait to get on the bus and continue learning Gracefall's song lineup. She was a quick study and had already mastered most, except for one solo, but she'd nail it soon.

Then there was being on stage. Cherry had sent her a tour schedule in which they had three shows booked in California. San Francisco, Los Angeles, and San Diego would be practice shows, then the tour would kick off in Arizona. She couldn't wait to show the guys what she was made of and battle it out with Jake on stage. Her fans, team Phoenix, were loyal and growing by the thousands. They even followed her from show to show.

The jet landed. As it was Elliot's turn to leave, she grabbed her carry-on, her prized Ibanez guitar, from the overhead compartment.

As she stepped off the private jet and onto the tarmac, Cherry, Gracefall's tour manager, quickly led her toward a row of four black and red Coach tour buses.

"How was your flight?" Cherry yelled over the roaring bus engines.

"Good." Elliot smiled.

"Good. Everyone is here, and once we get your luggage from the plane, we'll head out. Any questions for me?"

"No, I think I'm good."

"Well, if something comes up, text me. I'll be on the bus with the magicians who run the show." She pointed to the third bus in the row, and Elliot assumed it was the stage crew's ride. How else would the stage magically come together? From lighting to rig setup to sound engineering, these guys were the fireworks of the show. "Yours and Jake's bus is the second one."

"Great." Elliot smiled and made her way to her bus. She was excited to finally be here and get the tour started, but there was something else. No matter how hard she tried to suppress it, she couldn't stop the flutter in her stomach. She was excited to see Jake.

She opened the door to the bus and stepped inside. Two empty black leather couches sat in the lounge. "Hello."

Elliot was greeted by a shredding guitar coming from the back of the bus. She followed the sound, passing the kitchen and sleeping bunks, and found Jake sitting on another black couch, playing his Les Paul guitar. He nodded as he continued the riff.

She flashed him a peace sign as she set her guitar down, then removed her leather jacket.

Elliot listened closely, trying to hear Jake's influences in his playing. He had the speed and control of Eddie Van Halen and the in-your-face melody that reminded her of a Slash solo. Perhaps she'd underestimated the Pretty Boy. He had all the makings of a guitar hero.

Jake finished. "I was waiting for you to get here before I claimed a bunk. You can have the first pick."

"What a gentleman." Elliot chose a bottom bunk toward the front and laid her guitar and jacket inside. It was a decent twin bed with a swivel-out television. She unzipped the case, took out her Ibanez, and walked toward Jake. "You sound surprisingly good. After I get the gig, maybe I'll hire you as my guitar tech," she teased.

"Oh, how I've missed your smart ass."

"Aw, I'm flattered. You missed me." She plugged her guitar into the amp, then sat down next to Jake. "So, what are we playing?"

"I was going over the song list. You can pick it."

"Okay." She looked over the list, then began playing "Releasing Anger." The riff was one of her favorites from the late Moxley Sims. Jake joined in, adding the rhythm. They jammed together, finishing the song. After hearing Jake play, she needed to up her game. Together, they had matched chord for chord.

"Wow, you sound pretty good." Elliot laid her guitar on the couch next to her.

"I can hold my own." He flashed her a smile, and the flutter in Elliot's stomach came racing back. "So, are you ready for the tour?"

"Yeah." She rubbed her hands down her thighs as she looked around the bus. "This bus is sweet."

"Home away from home for the next six months." Jake leaned back, crossing his arms over his chest and stretching his long legs out in front of him.

Elliot leaned back as well and closed her eyes, breathing in his intoxicating bourbon and orange blossom scent. She had to admit, Jake looked good and was being way too nice to her. He'd be easier to hate if he wasn't such a nice guy. There had to be some skeletons in his closet. She just needed to find the fuckers and expose him for who he was.

"So, who are you leaving behind to follow the dream?" Jake asked.

Her heart tightened like someone had squeezed it. There was no way she was talking about her son. She wanted to, because it was just that easy to talk to Jake, but no. Eli was off-limits. "No one," she lied.

"Really? Not even a boyfriend?"

Yeah, he was definitely probing for information. Not today, pal. "Who has time for one of those? I don't." She turned her head toward Jake. "How about you? Does the missus know you'll be late for dinner?"

He laughed. "No girlfriend. However, I left the bar I co-own with my brother to be here."

"Really?" Intrigued with Jake's story, she rolled over on her side and tucked her legs under her. "You own a bar?"

"Yeah, my brother, Brian, and I opened the Tin Flask in

honor of our late father. He was killed in the line of duty. He was a police officer."

"Jake, I'm so sorry."

"Yeah, me too. He was a good guy."

"Well, the apple didn't fall far from the tree." What was she saying? Who had taken over her body?

Jake looked at her, shocked. "You think I'm a nice guy?"

"Maybe." She grinned.

"I thought I was the enemy."

"You are."

"I'm so confused."

They locked eyes. Charming blue eyes drew her in like a moth to a flame. Elliot should look away and get some distance from the enemy, but they were stuck on a tour bus together. Besides, Jake intrigued her. He was mysterious. With his talent, why wasn't he in a band? Underneath his calm, easy-going attitude, was there a rocker ready to be unleashed? If she was the betting type, she'd bet it all on red and say yes.

"Okay, Pretty Boy, I'll tell you one secret if you tell me one of yours."

"Sounds fair. Ladies first."

She exhaled. "Okay, here it goes. I was married to Dax Gage, the singer of Death Tribute."

"Really?"

"The worst two years of my life."

"How did that happen?"

"I was a hired gun for Death Tribute's Alice in Hell tour. They needed a guitarist. I needed a job. The rest is history."

"Given their reputation, I bet it was a wild ride."

"It was crazy. I got wrapped up in all the chaos. As soon as I left Dax, I got sober. It's been five years without a drink or drugs. Best decision of my life." And there she was, going down memory lane. Before she knew it, one secret had led to another.

"Wow! I'm impressed. You survived two years with Death Tribute. I'm way out of my league."

She laughed. "So, what about you, Pretty Boy?"

"I used to be a cop."

She sat up. "Get out!"

"Yep. Two years at the Reno PD until my father died in the line of duty." Jake broke their gaze. "I watched him die before the ambulance came."

"Oh, Jake," she gasped. "I can't even—"

"Yeah. After that, I quit the force."

The pain in his voice and grim expression were like a dagger to her heart. She reached out to touch his hand, then pulled back. She couldn't let her emotions get the best of her. "That was really cool of you to share that part of your life with me."

"You're easy to talk to." He flashed her a kind smile.

"Jake Quin, you are too good for rock and roll."

He shrugged. "We'll see."

A yawn escaped, and her eyes felt heavy. Tonight, they were playing their first practice show in San Francisco. She needed to rest before the show. "I'm going to take a nap." She sat up and rolled her neck from side to side, relieving the tension. "You should, too. It's going to be a long night."

"I'm good. Go get your beauty rest. I need to practice." He picked up his guitar, unplugging it from the amp, and began to strum.

"Suit yourself." As she made her way to her bunk, she didn't know what irritated her more. That he was a considerate, nice guy, which made it hard for her hate him, or the fact she was falling for the enemy.

7

Elliot and Jake's bus arrived at the venue in San Diego in time for soundcheck. Tonight's show was the last one before the actual tour started, which meant this was Elliot's last night to work out any kinks. On stage, she'd plugged right into the band with no problem. It was the solo on "Releasing Anger" she couldn't nail down. Technically, she was sound. The execution was off by a mile. Being this was Moxley's signature riff that fans loved, she couldn't mess it up.

"Hey, are you ready to go?" Jake asked as he scarfed down a Pop-Tart from the kitchen.

She shook her head. In the past week, Jake had gone through two boxes of Pop-Tarts. "You know those things are bad for a thirty-year-old man, right?"

"Lay off the tarts. You don't see me complaining about your rabbit food."

"Just wait until I start my workout routine. I start with a four-mile run, four times a week, and I'm bringing your ass with me." She poked his stomach, which was surprisingly muscular given the junk he ate. "Need to stay healthy on the road."

He lifted his black T-shirt, which fit him too perfectly, and patted his stomach. Elliot's eyes fixated on a narrow trail of dark hair below his navel. "I get plenty of exercise on stage, but I'll take you up on your offer. It's been a while since I've had to run down a suspect." He winked.

"I'll keep that in mind, Pretty Boy."

As she followed Jake to the door, her cell phone went off. She pulled it out of her back pocket and stared at the number.

Dax Gage.

Her heart dropped. She hadn't heard from Dax in three years. Someone was either calling to inform her that he was dead or was in the hospital dying. There was no other reason.

"Are you okay?" Jake asked.

"Yeah. Go ahead, and I'll catch up. I have to take this."

"Hello," she answered the call as Jake left the bus.

"Hey, baby." His deep voice was recognizable yet foreign to her.

"How did you get my number?"

"Does it matter?"

"Dax, I'm in no mood for your bullshit. I'm busy. Why are you calling?"

"I heard you're going on tour with Gracefall. Rock on, babe."

She wanted to believe that he was sincere, but she knew better. Dax only thought about himself. He wanted something.

"Look, I have soundcheck like now—"

"Right on. I thought maybe I'd pick up Elijah and go on a road trip and meet you at your next show."

"Hell no!"

"You can't keep me from my son. I have visitation rights."

"You lost your rights when you chose drugs over your son. Eli has seen you three fucking times since he was born."

"I know." His tone changed. "I fucked up, but I'm clean now, and I want to have a relationship with him."

Elliot couldn't trust what he was saying. She'd been burned too many times by the likes of Dax Gage.

"Can I at least come see you? I've missed you."

Tears welled in her eyes. There had always been a weak spot in her heart for Dax. She did love him at one time, but things had changed. She had changed, and Dax, well, was still Dax. "I can't do this."

"Come on, babe. We were good together."

"No, we were toxic together. Don't call me again." She hung up and took in a deep breath, calming her nerves. Her hands were shaking, and emotionally she was wrecked.

Was Dax going to push the issue to see his son? She didn't want to keep him from Eli, but she also wanted to keep Eli safe. Dax wasn't to be trusted. Knowing Dax, his intentions always benefited him, which made her think about how her career was taking off and his was self-destructing. Were there motives other than Dax wanting to see Eli? Was this about money?

Elliot was so confused and so late for soundcheck.

❧

*J*ake had been concerned when Elliot hadn't made it to soundcheck on time. Now he was even more worried watching her play like anything but The Phoenix. Her timing was off, and it looked like it was starting to irritate Dylan.

Before Jake knew what was happening, Dylan had stopped the song. "Elliot, what the hell?"

"I'm trying."

"Listen." Dylan placed a hand on his hip, the other holding the mic stand. "You were late for soundcheck, and now it's obvious you don't know the songs."

"I'm sorry I was late. It won't happen again."

"I don't think your mind is in it today. Sit this one out tonight." He tipped his chin toward Jake. "Jake will take over."

Wait...What?

Jake stood, shocked. Everyone has off days. Wasn't she allowed one, too?

"Are you serious?" She looked at Joe, then Tyler, and then Jake. They all stayed quiet.

"It's a privilege to be in this band. I can't put you on stage without you giving me one-hundred percent."

"I'll be fine. Come on, Dylan," Elliot pleaded.

"Take the night off, E. Get your shit together." Dylan got back to business. "Let's take it from the top."

The band played as Elliot strode off the stage.

What was going on with her? Jake's cop brain kicked in. This wasn't like her. What happened in the thirty minutes since he'd left her for soundcheck?

∾

*A*fter the show, Jake headed to the locker room to take advantage of a shower. Afterward, he'd meet back up with the guys in the green room, where they'd hang out and shoot the shit for a while before getting back on the bus. The show had been stellar. Dylan's vocals had been on point, even rocking the nosebleed section. Joe's drum solos had rattled the rafters. The whole experience of playing with Gracefall had been electric. He couldn't wait to kick off the tour. At first, he'd felt uncomfortable being on stage in front of thousands of people. Expectations were high, but once he tuned in with the band, the on-stage jitters went away.

Jake stripped out of his leather pants and stepped into the shower. He relaxed his sore muscles as the spray of the water rolled down his back. Elliot was right. He'd need to keep healthy out on the road if he was going to last six months.

Throughout the show, Jake couldn't shake the thought of Elliot being in some kind of trouble. Whatever it was, it had her alone on the bus, sitting on the sidelines. Dylan had dealt out some harsh punishment.

Jake quickly dried off and put on clean clothes before heading backstage to the green room. He would do a quick check-in with the guys, grab some food, then head to the bus to check on Elliot.

Inside the green room, Joe was on the phone, Dylan was lying on the couch, exhausted from the show, and Tyler was at the buffet table scarfing down the meat tray that catering had sent.

"Hey, Jake," Dylan sat up. "Kickass chops tonight, dude."

"You were on fire," Tyler agreed as he shoved a piece of rolled-up turkey into his mouth.

"Thanks. It felt really good." Jake grabbed a plate and started filling it with food, making sure he chose a few items Elliot would eat.

"So." Joe ended his call and joined Dylan on the couch.

"Just got off the phone with Davidson. He wants us to come up with some video concepts for 'Half Alive.'"

"I don't care what we do as long as I get to blow shit up," Tyler said as he joined the guys, sitting across from them in a beat-up leather chair.

"Since 'Half Alive' is a song about a breakup," Dylan began, "Let's go with a hot chick who breaks our hearts one at a time."

"Then, at the end, when we all find out that we've been played, we blow her up," Tyler added with a little more sincerity than Jake felt comfortable with.

"You're a sick fuck, T." Joe shook his head.

Tyler grinned, obviously owning his sick fuckery.

"How about a different approach?" Joe said, ignoring Tyler's suggestion. "Why don't we go with live footage from our shows?"

"Boring." Dylan pretended to yawn. "Hot chicks and rock stars. I'm telling you it's a proven hit method. Dudes want to be the rock star, and the chicks want to fuck the rock star. It's that simple."

"Yeah, the hot chick thing is a no-go for me," Joe said. "Mel wouldn't like it."

"Since when does Mel make decisions for the band? Don't be a pussy, dude."

"I'm not." Joe shoved Dylan. "I have respect for my fiancée."

"Why don't we ask Jake?" Tyler tipped his chin toward the guitarist.

Being put on the spot made Jake feel uncomfortable, and he choked on the piece of ham he'd just popped in his mouth. He was a nobody when it came to rock and roll. Chicks preferred rock stars, not studio musicians. "I wouldn't know. I don't have any groupies."

"I'll share." Tyler winked.

Jake ignored him. Knowing T's reputation of fucking anything in sight, he'd pass on the offer. "Besides, in six months, I might not be in the band."

"Shut the fuck up, dude." Dylan threw an empty beer can at him, and Jake dodged it in time before it landed on his plate. "You know you're in the band."

"Excuse me?" Joe shot Dylan a stern glare. "We haven't voted yet."

"Joe's right," Tyler chimed in. "I happen to think Elliot is amazing. We connect on stage. It's awesome."

"Listen," Jake interrupted. "I don't feel comfortable being here while you discuss band business. It's really not up to me."

Dylan stood and walked toward him. "No, Jake, I think you should tell us what you really think. I saw the way you reacted to me punishing Elliot for being late and fucking up."

Jake didn't know if it was the alcohol and drugs talking, or if he really was serious. "It was harsh the way you treated Elliot. She works her ass off, and I think if she's off one day, it's okay." Jake shrugged. "As far as a video goes, I like Joe's idea. You could make it a tribute to Moxley."

"I knew I liked him," Joe exclaimed.

Dylan shook his head, eyeing Jake suspiciously. "You like her, don't you?"

"What the fuck are you saying?" Jake had no idea where Dylan was going with this.

"Here's some friendly advice. Fuck Elliot and get her out of your system. Trust me, she'll fuck you over. They all do." Dylan pushed back the sweaty hair from his face as he left the room.

What the fuck? Jake stood speechless.

"Don't worry about it, Jake." Joe walked toward the buffet table where Jake was standing. "My brother is a cock bag. His ex-girlfriend is dating our band manager, and he's a little bitter about it."

"A little?" Jake complained.

"Yeah. We are thrilled to have both you and Elliot on tour with us." Joe squeezed his shoulder. "We're all still going through the emotions of losing Mox. I'm not making excuses for Dylan, but he's grieving the only way he knows how by being a dick."

"Yeah, I guess the band hasn't had much time to grieve."

"No, we haven't. If it weren't for my fiancée, I don't know what I'd do. She keeps me grounded."

"I get it. My dad died in the line of duty. He was a cop. His death was hard on my family. I don't think you really get over something like that."

"We all have our demons to deal with," Joe added, obviously not wanting to talk about it.

Jake nodded. "I should check on Elliot. She wasn't herself today."

"Yep." Joe picked up a plate as he surveyed the food table. "We should be rolling out of here soon. See ya in Arizona, bro."

Jake patted him on the back as he left the green room, heading toward the buses. He hoped Elliot was all right.

Balancing the plate of food piled with meats, cheeses, fruits, and vegetables, Jake unlocked the door and stepped inside the bus. He was greeted by a guitar solo coming from the back. "Elliot, I brought you some food."

She didn't hear him, so he headed to the back lounge to see what she was up to. Before he reached her, the solo ended, followed by cursing. Yeah, Elliot was having a terrible day.

He knocked on the sliding door that divided the bunks from the back lounge.

"Go away!" Elliot exclaimed as she started up the riff again.

Jake leaned his shoulder against the door. He could fix this if she would only let him. "I can help."

A series of fucks paraded from the room. From the sound of the screech coming from Elliot's guitar, she'd missed the chord again.

"I'm coming in." Jake opened the door. A lump formed in his throat. Elliot's eyes were red like she'd been crying. "Hey, are you okay?"

"I'm fine." Emotionally, she was closed off and hyper-focused on nailing the riff. Obviously, Elliot wasn't in the mood to talk, and he knew better than to push the issue. He took her guitar and sat down next to her. If she didn't walk to talk, she'd have to listen.

"It was a shitty thing Dylan did to you, but you can't let him win."

"I don't need your pep talk, Jake." She stood and began to walk away.

"Sit down," he said sternly in his cop voice. "Don't make me ask you again."

She turned and glared at him. He was thankful there wasn't anything around that could be used as a flying weapon because it would have been thrown in his direction.

"Don't be stubborn," he said more gently.

She plopped down next to him, and he played the part of the solo she was having trouble with. "You're so close. Right here, the chord changes, so the note changes." He slowed the riff down, showing her the change. "See?"

Elliot watched his fingers. "That's it?"

Jake nodded as he played the notes faster. "I told you, you were close." He handed her guitar back.

Elliot played the riff and played it perfectly.

"Thank you, Jake." The frustration lifted from her face. "But why would you help me? Why not let me struggle, so you have one up on me?"

"Because I like helping people. I'm not as bad as you think I am."

She diverted her gaze to the floor. "I guess I haven't been fair to you. You're not my enemy. Dax called me right before soundcheck. That's why I was late."

"I knew there had to be a good reason."

She looked up and took in a long breath, then slowly let it go. "Dax wants to see me."

Jake's heart plummeted. He knew he didn't have a shot with Elliot, but he was falling for her anyway. "Do you want to see him?"

"I don't. But there will always be a part of me that still loves him." Tears welled in her eyes as she looked at Jake. "I know. I'm pathetic."

"No, you're not. Trust me." Jake knew how she felt because he was still holding onto Stacy. Though, since he'd met Elliot, he hadn't given Stacy much thought. Jake wiped the tears away and held her face in his hands. Lightly, he caressed her cheeks as he gazed into her beautiful blue eyes. For a moment, her wall was down, and without saying a word, she let him in.

"It would be so easy to fall for you, Pretty Boy."

Jake flashed her a wicked smile. "I'm already there." He slid his hand to the back of her neck and pulled her into a kiss. It was a bold move, but fuck, he was tired of holding back. From the first time he saw her at the bar, he'd wanted to kiss her. Every time they were together he wanted to kiss her.

His tongue slid past her full lips and met with hers. She allowed him in as if she, too, had been wanting to kiss him. Slowly and passionately, he deepened the kiss. He could kiss her like this until the day he died and never tire, but she ended it.

She closed her eyes and rested her forehead against his. "I can't do this," she said breathlessly.

Jake knew it was too good to be true. Girls like Elliot didn't fall for good guys like him, which pissed him off. "Yeah." He pulled away. "You're right. This didn't feel right at all," he said sarcastically.

"Jake, please don't be like that." She clasped his arm. "I really like you."

"Great, that's the kiss of death. Next comes 'you're like a brother to me.'"

"Jake, that's not it."

Jake stood, his frustration getting the best of him. He faced Elliot. "Not all rockers are the enemy, Elliot. I'm really starting to care for you, you know."

"I know." She nervously picked at the cuticle around her fingernail. "I just think it's for the best we don't get involved."

Jake stood there for a moment, looking at her. He couldn't believe what she was saying. The whole situation felt like she was pushing him away. He wasn't delusional—he and Elliot had a connection. He nodded. "You're right."

She looked up at him, apparently shocked that he was giving up so easily.

"We can't afford to bring our hearts into this competition. Our focus should be on the prize." He folded his arms.

"Yeah." She stood and met him eye to eye. "I totally agree."

"Good. Now that we got that out of the way, I'm going to bed." He turned and headed toward the bunks.

"You're cute when you're sulking, Pretty Boy," she teased as she followed him to the bunks.

"I'm not sulking," he exclaimed, climbing into his bunk.

"Yes, you are." She climbed into her bunk across from his.

"Go to sleep." He closed the curtain and lay down.

"Sweet dreams, Pretty Boy."

Jake smiled to himself. She was totally playing hard to get, but two could play that game.

8

*E*lliot sat on the edge of her bunk, tying her running shoes. They had been on the road for two days, and the bus had arrived at the Texas venue late last night, giving her the morning to go for a run. Most mornings, she had to settle for yoga in the back lounge, but not today. She couldn't wait to breathe in the fresh air and get her heart pumping. Three weeks had been the longest she'd gone without a run.

Elliot headed toward Jake's bunk, where he was still sleeping. "Hey." She shoved his shoulder. "Wake up, Pretty Boy. We're going for a run."

Jake moaned and rolled onto his back.

"I told you to be careful partying with Whiplash." As soon as they had pulled in last night, Whiplash, their opening act, had thrown a party on their bus. She'd bet she was the only one up at six o'clock this morning.

"What time is it?" Jake wiped the sleep from his eyes.

"It's time for a run." She tore the sheets off him and took a step back, taking in his ripped chest. It didn't matter how many times she'd seen him half-naked on stage, backstage, or on the bus; the urge to feel his body against hers was always there.

"Hey!" He sat up and grabbed her waist, pulling her on top of him.

She squealed. The bunk was low, making it easy for Jake to pull her against him. She straddled him, placing her hands on his chest, fighting his hold on her. "You smell like a brewery."

"My head is still buzzing." His hands rested on her hips. That wasn't the only thing buzzing. Through his boxers and her yoga pants, she felt his hard cock pressing against her sex. *Fuck!*

She gazed down at him. Even with disheveled hair and hungover, he was sexy. "Who were you dreaming of?"

"A gorgeous blonde with blue catlike eyes." He yawned, still half asleep.

"Ohhh, she sounds hot." Fucking with Jake was too much fun. He had no idea what he was saying or doing.

"You have no idea." In a half-drunk daze, he gradually moved his hands onto her ass and squeezed. "Elliot, your ass is amazing."

She should tell him to remove his hands from her butt, but he felt too good. She moved her hips forward, loving the feel of his cock against her sex. She bent down and whispered in his ear. "Oh, you are so going to hate me."

"Why is that?"

"You're going on a run with me."

"No, I'm not," he moaned as he continued squeezing her ass.

"Yes, you are."

"It will take an act from God to get me out of this bed."

"I'll make a deal with you. If you catch me, I'll let you kiss me." She pinned him with a flirty pirate smile.

Jake tossed her aside. "Give me ten." He got up, making a dash toward the bathroom.

Elliot lay back, propping herself up by her elbows, and laughed. "Hey, what's your end of the deal? What do I get if I catch you?"

Jake came around the corner, tugging his T-shirt over his head. "I'll let you kiss me." He winked and flashed her a smile.

~

*H*alf a mile into her run, Elliot was midway around the outside of the stadium, which looked like a futuristic spaceship. This early in the morning, no one was outside, so she could peacefully work out her muscles without being seen by fans. She breathed in the fresh air, pushing herself to finish the lap.

Somewhere between the south gate and the front entrance of the stadium, she'd lost Jake. She laughed. There was no way he was catching up to her, which really didn't matter. Either way, she was getting a kiss.

Fighting the feelings she had for Jake was more challenging than she'd thought. The last show they'd played together proved that Jake was sincerely a nice guy when he invited a young boy from the audience to play with the band. He had given the little dude his guitar, and he shredded it like a pro. Jake was great with kids, which made her think about Eli. Her son deserved a man like Jake in his life. Not a monster like Dax.

Since she'd met Jake, she'd known better than to think she could play alone. He made her want to break all the rules and go for it. But no. It was too risky for her to trip and fall in love. Nor was playing house with Jake on her bucket list. All that mattered was getting the gig.

So, no matter how much she'd wanted to explore Jake's body this morning when he was pressed against her, making her ache with need, she wasn't falling into lust. Yeah, she loved the feeling, wanted to be with someone again, but she had to be strong. Anyhow, it was just one kiss.

Even if she wanted to let Jake in, emotionally, she couldn't. She'd been all in with Dax. She'd trusted him with her heart, which had been an enormous mistake. It had taken hours of therapy to rid herself of Dax, yet the threat of slipping back into her old ways was only a drink away. Knowing eventually she'd have to face him brought back old memories she'd rather forget. Dax was unpredictable, and for that reason alone she couldn't bring Jake into her drama.

Stick to the plan.

Elliot reached the entrance to the stadium and found Jake waiting for her.

"What's this?" she said, catching her breath.

"Catching up to you." Jake's face was flushed and sweaty. He was heaving and coughing as he breathed. Yeah, totally out of shape.

"Did you cheat?" She placed her hands on her hips, still taking in much-needed air.

"No." He struggled to breathe. "I took a shortcut."

"You cheated. There is no way you beat me."

"Call it what you want. You never said I couldn't use a shortcut. By the way, there's a sweet breakfast spread in the green room."

"So, you stopped and grabbed a snack?"

"No, I thought we'd go and check it out."

She shook her head and followed him inside the stadium. "You are so bad."

The rush of cold air hitting her sweaty skin and clothes was welcomed. Texas heat was brutal, even this early in the morning.

As they made their way to the dressing room, they passed all sorts of Dallas Cowboys banners and logos. A massive lone-star light fixture hung from the industrial-style ceiling as they passed the lower-level concession stands. There was a stadium club restaurant, which was closed. Everywhere you looked, you knew this was the home of the Dallas Cowboys.

"This place is impressive," Jake said as he took it all in.

Elliot gazed at the ceiling in awe. "I bet it looks amazing at night all lit up."

"Well, we'll find out tonight."

"I can't wait."

They reached the locker room, and Jake opened the door for her, which was nice and annoyed her at the same time. She couldn't believe she was standing inside the Dallas Cowboys Cheerleaders locker room. She was sure it was upon the request of Dylan that their dressing room would be the cheerleaders' locker room.

It was pretty nice. The walls were lined with wooden cubbies and steel lockers labeled with each cheerleader's name in bright blue-and-silver letters. They were all empty except the last six cubbies, which were designated for the members of Gracefall. Her clothes, shoes, and toiletry bag had taken over Kelsey's locker. "Hey, look." She nodded toward the locker. "We're all Dallas Cowboys Cheerleaders." She laughed.

"Hell, yeah. Who am I?" Jake didn't have to search long. His stuff was next to hers. "Sweet! I'm Kelly."

Elliot walked over to the buffet table set up in the middle of the room. Fruits, bagels, cereals, and chafing dishes filled with eggs, bacon, and pancakes were spread out. Fresh breakfast mimosas caught her eye at the end of the table. Jake wasn't kidding; this was amazing.

She opened a bottle of water, enjoying the coldness as she felt Jake's eyes on her. She turned around, and he was standing behind her, way too close. His smoldering gaze met hers, and all she could think was *oh shit.*

No, this isn't happening.

"I'm ready to cash in on the deal." Jake cocked a half-smile that twisted her with need.

She clenched the cold water bottle to her chest, trying to cool down her overheated hormones. "What deal? You cheated." She ignored the pull of his seductive charm.

"The rules were never clearly stated, so I still get a kiss." He took the water bottle from her hand and set it down on the table.

"Jake, I can't do this."

"Then tell me to leave." He moved in closer. His lips lightly brushed against hers. "Tell me to leave, Elliot, and I will."

The words lodged in her throat as he cradled her face, bringing her into a hot, passionate kiss. God, he tasted good. The urge to plunge her tongue deeper into his wet, hot mouth was too much. She pulled back, controlling the sexual chaos unfolding inside her.

"Elliot, please don't push me away." He caressed her cheek as he gazed deeply into her eyes. "I know you want to let me in."

A tear slid down her face. She hadn't realized until right now the extent of Dax's damage. Why couldn't she just let go?

"Jake," a whispered protest escaped her lips. Letting Jake in was a reckless move, but damn, he left her defenseless. This was more than attraction. Something more powerful pulled her to Jake. She almost believed she could trust him.

He took her hand and walked toward the showers.

"Umm, what are we doing?"

He looked over his shoulder at her. "We're taking a shower."

Her body went rigid, and her heart raced. "Shower? As in we're getting naked?" That definitely was a bad idea.

He stopped by his locker and picked up a bottle of soap and shampoo. "Usually you're naked, unless you shower with clothes on." He shrugged. "It's up to you."

"Hold on." She planted her feet. "I'm not getting naked with you."

"We both need a shower. What are you scared of, Elliot?" With one look, he consumed her. His sexy blue gaze shot through her body like a bolt of lightning. She couldn't resist him.

They continued to the showers, passing a wall lined with a slab of white marble that housed five sinks, each with its own lighted mirror. The air hitched in Elliot's throat when she saw the stalls. There was one substantial, open, tiled stall with no privacy. Each showerhead protruding out of the wall was designated for one person. As she did the calculations, that meant at least ten cheerleaders could fill the shower at a time. No wonder guys went crazy over women's locker rooms.

Jake took off his shirt and slipped off his shorts. He tipped his chin at her. "What are you waiting for?" He flashed her a wicked grin as he walked over to the faucet and turned it on.

He looked confident, while she was nervous, but she

wouldn't let him know that. He had something up his sleeve. She'd play along. She tugged her shirt off, then bent down and rolled her yoga pants and underwear down her legs, kicking them off to the side. She grabbed two towels from the rack, then made her way to Jake.

~

*J*ake watched Elliot set the towels aside, then stand in front of him with her hands on her hips, completely comfortable with being naked. "Clothes are so overrated." She gave him a full view of her body.

Fuck yeah, they were. Elliot was gorgeous. She worked out, and it showed in her toned stomach and muscular legs and arms. Her skin was flawless, except for a brown birthmark on her right hip.

"Come here." He took her hand and led her into the shower. "You don't mind if we share, do you?"

"As long as that's all we do." She tested the water with her hands before stepping into the spray. "I'm not having sex with you, Pretty Boy."

"It never crossed my mind." *Liar.*

She gave him the side-eye. "I don't know how you talked me into this."

"There was no convincing." He stood behind her, catching some of the water and sneaking a peek at her ass. Her round, full ass would fit perfectly in his hands. From this view, it was going to be hard not to think about sex. Sex wasn't the goal here. The only way Elliot would trust him was if he showed her.

He unleashed her hair from her ponytail, then poured

shampoo in his hand. Gently, he massaged her scalp, bringing the soap to a lather. "How does that feel?"

"Fucking amazing." She tipped her head back. "Are you sure you haven't worked at a salon as the shampoo boy?"

Jake laughed. "No, but I can make you a drink and play you a song."

"Hmm, sounds like a date," she teased.

He moved her under the shower to rinse her hair. "Someday, I'd like to take you out on a date."

She wiped the water from her face. "Don't you think that's a bad idea?"

"Not at all." Jake stepped under the shower, wetting his hair.

"Well, it's reckless. We should be focused on the gig."

Water dripped from his hair and down his face as his gaze narrowed onto hers. She was doing it again, pushing him away, hiding behind an excuse. He approached her, keeping a small distance between them. "I'm not buying it, Elliot. There's something between us, and I know you feel it, too."

"It doesn't matter." She looked away. "It just can't be."

"I think it can. If you let me in." He cupped her cheek, brushing his thumb over her bottom lip. "Elliot, you're more than a pretty face to me. You're a strong, independent woman. I like that."

"No, I'm far from strong and independent." Tears welled in her eyes. "I wish I had met you sooner, before Dax. Then maybe I wouldn't be so broken."

At this moment, he'd never hated anyone more than Dax Gage. His name alone sent a bolt of rage through his body. He wished he could erase him entirely from her past. "What did he do to you?"

She shook her head. "Jake—"

"You don't have to tell me. But you can talk to me when you're ready."

Her body began to tremble as tears streamed down her face. The sorrow in her eyes left Jake feeling helpless, hatred toward Dax growing. If the bastard walked into the room right now, he'd knock the fucker out.

He held her, and she didn't push him away. Instead, she exhaled and fell into his embrace, holding onto him like a lifeline. She sobbed uncontrollably as if she were releasing years of heartache and pain. He kissed the top of her head. "That's it, baby, let it all go. I got you."

If it made her feel better, Jake would hold her forever. He knew he couldn't fix what had been broken, but he'd work like hell to mend the pieces. She deserved as much. He tightened his grip, and she exhaled a shaky breath. "I'm so sorry for whatever Dax has done to you. There's a special kind of hell for assholes like that."

His heart sank deeper into his stomach as she looked up at him with tears in her eyes. "You don't have to apologize, Jake. Thank you for understanding and just being here."

"I'm always here for you, Elliot." He brushed her wet hair from her forehead. She needed to smile. "Just for the record, taking a shower with a hot chick is the hardest thing I've done. And I was a cop."

She giggled, and there was that infectious smile of hers that Jake loved. "I'm impressed," she teased.

"Really?" He sounded more surprised than he should have been. He'd considered himself well built, attractive. But to impress the likes of Elliot Phoenix? That was a different story. Jokingly, he puffed out his chest. Her compliment was a total ego booster.

She rolled her eyes and gave him a crooked grin. "Now you're just being an egomaniac."

"Well, at least I made you laugh."

A comfortable silence settled between them. Jake caressed her cheek with the back of his knuckles; her skin was soft. He leaned in a pressed his lips against hers, nudging her mouth open with his tongue, kissing her slowly and thoroughly. He didn't want to push it too far; she'd cracked the door open and allowed him to see a vulnerable side of her, and he didn't want to ruin the little trust he'd gained.

The kiss continued down her neck. She tipped her head back, giving him more to explore with his tongue. Holding back was difficult. She tasted too damn good. Sweet moans and soft skin. *Fuck!*

"Jake." The way she said his name had him hanging on by a thread. "You feel amazing, but we should stop."

The kiss stopped, and he nuzzled her neck. "Yeah, you're probably right."

She slipped out of his embrace and shut off the water. Then she turned and faced him. "Why are you so easy to talk to?"

"Because I'm a good listener." Jake shook his head like a dog.

"Oh, shit!" Jake heard Tyler from the doorway. "I'm sorry. I didn't know anyone was in here."

Jake's body tensed. He pulled Elliot behind him, shielding her from Tyler's eyes. "Yeah. Um." He rubbed the back of his neck. "We're just finishing up."

"Hey." Tyler raised his hands in front of him. "I didn't see a thing."

"It's not like that," Elliot said, glaring at Tyler over Jake's shoulder.

"Look, it's none of my business." Tyler backed out of the shower room slowly. "Nice ass, Elliot."

A shampoo bottle flew from Elliot's direction, almost hitting Tyler before he left the room.

"Fuck, this isn't good." Elliot grabbed a towel and wrapped it around her body.

"Don't worry. Everything will be fine." At least he hoped so.

Elliot tossed him a towel. "Jake, if Tyler says something, it could cost us the gig."

"I don't think so." Jake dried his hair before he wrapped the towel around his waist.

"I have to go and talk with him about this."

He pulled her into his embrace before she had a chance to leave. "Hey, you're freaking out."

"Damn right I am. I can't lose this gig." She tried to pull away, but he held her closer.

"Elliot, look at me." She did. "Breathe." Jake inhaled, making her do the same, then he exhaled, motioning for her to repeat it. "Everything will be fine. I'll talk to Tyler. The only way you're losing this gig is if it's to me." He tried to joke, but she was apparently in no mood when she hit him with a look that could kill.

"Trust me. I'll talk to Tyler. Everything will be fine."

God, he hoped so. If not, he'd just royally screwed up.

9

*J*ake and the rest of Gracefall stood in front of eighty thousand screaming fans as they finished their encore. The energy in the stadium was electric, like nothing he'd ever experienced. He'd fed off the excitement, showing off his guitar licks and feeling like a rock star.

There were still a few diehard Moxley Sims fans who'd show up at shows. They'd turn their backs to Jake during his solos, making it known that the great Moxley would never be replaced. However, by the end of the show, Jake would always prove them wrong. He could play with the big dogs.

As he took a bow, throwing a few guitar picks into the crowd, he couldn't believe it. He was living the dream, and it felt fucking amazing. Better than mind-blowing sex. Well, a close second. He wished his father could see him now. He'd be proud.

Riding the rock and roll rush was like a drug racing through his veins. He craved nights like this on stage performing for thousands of fans. This is what he wanted to do for the rest of his life.

Dylan put his arm around Jake, and they both took a bow. "Dude, you've got your pick." Dylan pointed to the front row of groupies. "Which one are you fucking tonight?"

"I'm good." Jake handed his guitar off to his tech.

"I think you should pick the blonde," Elliot said as she passed by.

Fuck yeah, he'd fuck the blonde that had just walked by him in skin-tight black leather pants and a rock concert tank.

Since they'd met, Jake had been confused about where he stood with Elliot. One minute they were flirting, the next she was cold as ice. He'd given her space. Well, as much as he could since they were bus mates. He needed to step up his game, but knew he needed to tread softly.

Backstage was chaotic. The fans were still cheering, feeding Jake and the rest of the band's adrenaline high, as Cherry rushed them down the hallway to the green room. Cherry barked out instructions, but all Jake heard over the slowly disappearing crowd's cheers was an after-show party. He didn't care where the party was, as long as Elliot was there.

An hour later, Jake was showered and tying his boots, dressed in his black jeans and army-green t-shirt.

"You ready to go, Pretty Boy?"

Jake looked up at Elliot's smokey catlike eyes. She was fucking beautiful in tight black leather pants and a leather jacket that was zipped down enough to show off a peek of her breasts. The outfit was simple, yet she looked like a million bucks. Her hair was down with a slight curl.

"Is there something wrong?" Elliot looked over her outfit. "Should I change?"

He cleared his throat, giving himself time to get it together. "Hell no. You look amazing." He looked down, continuing to tie his boot as if she hadn't just sent his hormones into a tailspin. After seeing her naked this morning, all he'd thought about was when he'd see her naked again...and there would be a next time.

He stood, nonchalantly trying to adjust and hide the fact he wanted her. They walked out of the green room and followed the band to the after-show party.

Elliot yawned. "God, what I wouldn't do to be on the bus sleeping right now. I feel like I haven't slept in days. How are you holding up?"

"I'm good. Pumped." Jake flashed his metal horns.

"You looked good out there tonight." She gave him a sideways glance, then winked.

"Really?"

She shoved his shoulder. "No, I'm fucking with you," she teased.

Jake smiled. "I knew something was up."

"Maybe you don't know how to take a compliment." She gave him a sly, sexy grin.

Devin, the lead singer from Whiplash, and Misti, their drummer, came up behind them. Jake felt Misti slap his ass. "What's up, hot stuff?"

Devin put his arm around Elliot. "You guys rocked it tonight." His eyes traveled to Elliot's tits. "Gracefall treating you good?"

"It's going good," Jake said, not liking the way the lead singer was hanging all over Elliot.

"Devin, stop drooling all over Elliot's tits." Misti rolled her eyes as she stayed in step with Jake. "You know he's been dying to meet Elliot Phoenix, and this is how he acts." She shook her head. "Uncool, dude."

Playfully, Devin wiggled his tongue up and down in true rocker fashion.

"Eww." Elliot pushed Devin's arm off her. "Anyone who has to show off their tricks must be lacking in other areas." She glanced at Devin's package. "False advertising. I bet it's a sock."

Misti belted out a laugh as she and Elliot walked ahead.

"I like this view better." Devin held out his fist for Jake to bump as he gawked at the girls' asses.

Jake wasn't touching Devin's hand. It would be like shaking the hand of a venereal disease. Hello, hand sanitizer, anyone?

Joe, Tyler, and Dylan walked into the stadium club restaurant first while the four of them followed. Instantly, all eyes were on them. People surrounded them, shaking their hands, asking for an autograph, and snapping pictures. He could only assume they were employees from the record company since Clef Tonic was throwing the party.

Jake got pulled aside by two young ladies in spandex dresses asking for a photograph as a waitress popped over, handing out the champagne. Everything happened so fast, he'd lost track of his bandmates and Elliot.

Jake stood between the ladies. One held a cell phone out for a selfie while the other had her hands all over him.

"Jake Quin, how does it feel to be famous?" one of the girls purred.

He looked down at her and winked. "Fucking amazing."

Before Jake knew what was happening, Cherry was pulling him away from the groupies. "He's mine, ladies."

Jake followed Cherry to the VIP section. "You're welcome," Cherry said over her shoulder. "Those two would chew you up and spit you out."

"Yeah, thanks," Jake yelled over the loud music.

Cherry led him to her entourage at the end of the bar.

Kimmy smiled and waved him over to where she was hanging out with Elliot and Melody.

"Jake!" Kimmy greeted him excitedly with a big drunken hug. "Come hang with us." She grabbed his hand and pulled him toward the group.

He stood next to Elliot, and she tipped her chin to the two groupies. "Who knew you were the ladies' man?"

He took a step closer to Elliot away from Kimmy and the others. "Jealous?"

She shrugged. "Depends."

"On what?"

"Who you're bringing back to the bus." Jake watched Elliot bring her glass of water to her lips. Christ, what he wouldn't do to kiss her.

"Hmm?" Jake gazed across the room as if he were searching for a hot chick to take back to the bus. He turned and faced Elliot. "I have my eyes on this extremely sexy blonde."

Elliot gave him a teasing smile as if she knew he was talking about her. "Sounds hot."

"And she's a guitar goddess."

Elliot laughed. "Jake, is that the best pickup line you got? Guitar goddess?"

"Okay." He leaned against the bar, making sure no one was looking at them. Pinning her with his best smoldering gaze, he traced the zipper of her leather jacket with his finger. "Roses are red, violets are blue. How would you like it if I came home with you?"

Elliot's head flew back as she laughed harder than last time. "Oh, you're cute."

Jake shrugged and straightened. "I aim to please."

"Hey, you guys, what's so funny?" Melody asked. She

extended a hand to Jake. "Remember me from the club? I'm Joe's fiancée."

"Lucky bitch," Kimmy teased as she sipped her fruity drink through a straw and swayed to the music thumping through the speakers.

"Right." Jake shook her hand. "That's right. I met you at The Black Veil a few months back."

"Yep. How's it going? Elliot was just telling us about the chemistry you guys have on stage."

He glanced at Elliot, who was wide-eyed and looking extremely uncomfortable. "Umm...you know...like how well we play off each other."

It amused him the way her cheeks were turning a light red.

"They are freaking hot together on stage," Cherry added. "You'd think they were a couple."

Jake and Elliot shared a knowing smile. And there was the hope he needed to see. He gazed deep into her eyes as he responded. "I only play with the best." He winked.

A heavy look formed in her eyes, and he knew at once he'd nailed the pickup line, securing a night alone with Elliot.

"Well, a word of advice." Kimmy set her drink on the bar and motioned to the bartender to bring another. "Don't fall for the enemy. Both of you are competing for a once-in-a-lifetime opportunity. Don't fuck it up."

For Kimmy being tipsy, she was a real buzzkill.

"Well, on that note." Jake pushed off the bar. "I'll leave you ladies and go hang with the dudes."

"I didn't mean to sound like a bitch, Jake." Kimmy reached out and grabbed his arm.

"No worries."

"Hey," Melody interrupted. "If you see Joe, tell him I'm waiting." She winked. "He'll know what I mean."

Jake flashed the peace sign and walked away.

Fuck, sex was pulsing in the air tonight. Never in a million years would Jake have seen himself talking to four sexy, beautiful girls at one time. It was hard enough to speak to one.

At the other end of the bar, Tyler was ordering a drink. Jake joined him.

Tyler turned and looked at him. "Hey, brother, what's your poison tonight?"

"Bourbon."

"Good choice." Tyler got the bartender's attention. "Two bottles of Widow Jane bourbon."

"So, about this morning with Elliot in the shower—"

"Fuck you, bro." Tyler shook his head. "I told you already; I didn't see a thing."

"I know, but—"

"But nothing."

The bartender returned with two bottles of bourbon. Tyler took one and handed it to Jake. "Fucking rock and roll," he exclaimed, clinking his bottle with Jake's.

They both tossed back a long shot. Jake coughed at the aftereffects of the amber liquid burning his throat, which was raw from singing backup vocals. He wasn't used to it, but he found himself doing it a lot, depending on the type of mood Dylan was in.

"Pussy." Tyler thew back another sip.

"Not as young as I once was." He coughed.

Tyler turned around, facing the crowded room. "Yeah, rock and roll will age you like a mofo. I'm thirty-two and feeling like sixty."

"Thirty is still young." Jake joined him and turned around for the same view. "We're in our prime."

"How's that?"

"We're at the age when we finally know what we want. We've had our twenties to fuck up. You know, get shit out of our system."

"If you're talking about settling down and starting a family," Tyler gave him the side-eye, "then fuck off."

Jake shrugged. "No man, I'm talking about knowing who you are and knowing what you want."

Tyler shook his head. "Bro, you're way too deep. I just want to get drunk and fuck."

They tapped their bourbon bottles again and silently agreed to disagree.

"Rock and roll." Jake tipped the bottle.

"Jake!" He heard Dylan belting out his name in his screamer rocker vocals that he was almost sure would break glass. Joe was behind him with a beer in hand.

Dylan leaned in, giving him a bro hug. "Bourbon. Oh, hell yeah, dude!" He got the bartender's attention and pointed at Jake's Widow Jane.

Joe took a seat next to Jake, resting his elbows on the table. He didn't make eye contact as he tossed his beer back. "You freakin' killed it tonight," he said in an even tone, almost like it pained him to acknowledge his playing. "Mox would be proud."

Jake didn't know how to react to Joe's statement. He knew it was tough for Joe, seeing him play Moxley's riffs and solos. He was overjoyed that he was nailing the music, but fuck, Moxley's ghost was forever haunting his ass.

"That means a lot, Joe."

"You're damn right it does." Joe continued to stare at the bottles on the shelf behind the bar.

"Oh, before I forget." Which he almost did as the bourbon assaulted his brain. "Melody said she's waiting or something like that."

Joe's whole body perked up. He faced Jake. "Where is she?"

Jake pointed to the end of the bar.

"Fuck yeah." Joe shot out of the barstool and strode toward Melody. Jake watched them as they locked eyes, madly in love. Melody's face glowed, smiling at Joe as he went to kiss her. Jake could only wish that one day Elliot would look at him like that.

He glanced at Elliot, and she, too, was looking at the happy couple. Was she thinking about him? Was she wishing that he'd walk up to her and claim her in front of everyone? Fuck, he was drowning in the alcohol.

"Dude, are you okay?" Dylan asked as he grabbed his bottle of bourbon off the table.

"Yeah." Jake shook off the thought of Elliot, but his eyes were still on her as he watched a tall, well-built man with tattoos covering his arms walk up to Elliot and kiss her cheek. The look on her face showed she'd been caught off guard.

The guy flipped his long dirty-blond hair back, and Jake caught a glimpse of his face. From the pictures he'd seen of Death Tribute, that was Dax Gage.

His body went rigid as rage filled his veins. Jake had never met the guy, but he hated him for what he'd done to Elliot. He fisted his hands as Dax put his arm around Elliot. It was apparent she was uncomfortable by the way she tried to avoid him, throwing his arm off her.

It took all his might not to rush Dax and knock him on his ass. Never had he wanted to hurt someone as badly as he wanted to hurt Dax. He wanted him to feel Elliot's pain.

Fuck!

What was wrong with him? He shoved his hand through his hair. He wasn't one to start fights, nor had the thought crossed his mind to hurt someone before, but for Elliot, he would.

Jake stood there watching until Dax grabbed her arm, and Elliot looked scared. *Fuck that.*

He took a gulp of bourbon liquid courage set it down, then started toward the end of the bar when Dylan stopped him. "Is she worth it, dude?"

Jake was taken back. Had it been that obvious? "Yes, Elliot's in trouble."

"That's her ex. Do you really want to get involved?"

Did he? Regardless of his hatred toward the man, Dax was making Elliot uncomfortable. He was here to serve and protect. "What the fuck? Yes!" Jake was getting testy and feeling bulletproof. "He's harassing her."

Dylan looked at Elliot, then back at Jake. "Okay. Let's do this."

"Wait." Jake held Dylan back. "This isn't your fight."

"Fuck yeah, it is, dude. That's our guitarist. She's family."

"Shit." Tyler interrupted, overhearing the conversation. "I was hoping to get laid, but family is family." He turned to face the group at the end of the bar. "Who are we fucking up?"

Jake pointed to Dax.

Tyler cracked his knuckles. "That dude's an asshole. Met him once, and that was enough for me."

"Just stay here," Jake demanded. "I'll go check out the situation. I'll call for backup if needed." Fuck, he sounded like a cop.

Jake made his way to Elliot. The relief on her face when

she saw him made him feel like a hero coming to rescue the damsel in distress.

"Hey." He tapped Dax on the shoulder. "Everything all right here?" Yep, his old cop days were coming back. He looked at Elliot. "You okay?"

"Jake, I'm fine." She sounded meek, like she didn't want any trouble.

"Who's this?" Dax asked as if Jake was the pesky fly in the room.

"Dax, this is Jake. Jake, Dax." Elliot gave the introduction as though she really didn't want to. To say the situation was awkward would be an understatement.

"So, you're Jake. Elliot's competition." Dax tipped his head back, flipping his blond hair and letting his ego show. "I'd have thought Gracefall could find better talent."

Jake inhaled, trying to keep calm, but it wasn't working.

"I mean, seriously, we all know chicks can't play guitar," Dax snorted.

"Okay." Elliot stepped in. "That's enough, Dax. Stop fucking around." She turned Dax around and was ready to push him away from the situation when Jake stopped her.

"Elliot, he's a grown man. If he's got something to say, let him say it." Jake puffed out his chest as he advanced on Dax, giving him the stare down.

"Don't do this, Jake." Elliot tried to break up the tension, but Cherry held her back.

"Elliot, let them have their pissing battle," Cherry said as she held Elliot's arm, moving her away from the scene.

Jake made a rookie mistake and took his eyes off the enemy. He glanced at Elliot to make sure she was okay when suddenly he felt Dax's fist clock him in the face, almost taking him down.

Jake wiped the blood from his lip. "Cheap shot."

Dax stood with hands in front of him like he was Mohammed Ali, ready to fight. "You want more, asshole?"

A wicked smile spread across Jake's lips. "Fuck yeah, I do." The leash holding him back snapped, and Jake charged Dax, spearing him in the stomach like he'd seen professional wrestlers do. They stumbled backward as fists hit flesh in a chaotic fury.

He'd gotten a few good hits in until Dax landed an uppercut, sending stars bursting behind his eyelids. He blinked back the darkness. Where the fuck was his backup?

They rammed into tables, sending chairs flying in all directions. People scattered, desperately keeping out of their way. He heard Elliot yelling at Dax to stop, then Cherry screaming at him. Their words became muffled by rage as he continued to fight.

His backup rushed in, trying to separate them. Dax let up and backed away, wiping his bloody nose as Dylan and Tyler pushed Jake away from Dax.

As he calmed himself down, Elliot raced over to Dax, checking his wounds. What the fuck? Why didn't she come to him?

With his heart crushed and completely confused, he shook free from Dylan and Tyler's hold. "I'm fine." He wiped his mouth as he stared at Elliot. She glared back. Was she mad at him?

Cherry stepped in front of him. "I'm getting you out of here before the press sees this."

"I'm leaving on my own." He shrugged Cherry off and walked away, grabbing his bourbon bottle on the way out.

What the hell was going on?

10

*A*fter the commotion, Elliot left the party and headed back to the bus. She was done with Dax playing the victim. Jake would have never hit him if he hadn't been an asshole. But that was Dax. She'd wanted to leave with Jake, but the situation with Dax was complicated. He held her son over her like a hostage, and that was something she had to tread softly around. She couldn't chance pissing Dax off and him taking Eli away from her. He'd already pressed the fact he wanted to see him.

Quietly, she slipped inside the bus, careful not to alert Jake she was there. The slider door that separated the sleeping bunks from the back of the bus was shut. Soft strokes from a guitar played.

Jake.

The music soothed her as she made her way to her bags in one of the junk bunks. With only her, Jake, and the bus driver on the bus, there was lots of storage. She found it comical how she and Jake's special guitars had their own bunks.

She smiled and shook her head as she grabbed a pair of

boxers and a tank top to sleep in, then retreated to the bathroom to change, remove her makeup, and brush her teeth. Getting out of tight leather pants was a dream come true, even though she loved her leather pants. They made her ass look amazing. Really, she loved anything leather. She loved the smell of it, the softness of it. It was just so rock and roll.

Ten minutes later, Elliot left the bathroom and put her stuff away. She walked to her bunk, ready to climb in, then paused. She needed to check on Jake. No, she wanted to check on Jake but was too embarrassed by Dax's actions tonight. Jake had done the right thing. She'd felt uncomfortable when Dax grabbed her arm, insisting that they go somewhere private to chat. Elliot was okay with talking. But being alone with Dax? No way. She wasn't slipping back into old bad habits.

She'd been clean for five years. Eli had been her strength as she pulled herself out of the gutter and broke free from that awful mistake. Dax had ruined her career, body, and soul. Love had made her blind and foolish. The worst part was she'd allowed it to happen.

Elliot walked down between the bunks to the back of the bus, fixing her ponytail high on her head. What was she going to say to him? Maybe a peace offering would help break the ice. Quickly, she padded back to the refrigerator and grabbed two bottles of water and his favorite breakfast item, Pop-Tarts.

She tapped on the slider door.

"Go away." His voice sounded raspy and deep, as though he had a stuffy nose.

"Jake, it's me." She didn't blame him for not wanting to see her, but fuck it. Living in tight quarters, they needed to clear the air. "I'm coming in." She pulled the slider back, and Jake was sitting on the black leather couch with his head back and his guitar on his lap, strumming it lightly. A bottle of bourbon, a quarter of the way gone, sat next to him. He sat up, and Elliot had to hold back the laughter. Two tissues half-soaked with blood hung from his nose. When she noticed the blood, she stopped laughing. "Jake, I'm so sorry."

"Don't feel a thing," he slurred.

"You will in the morning." She leaned against the doorframe, taking him in. He still wore the clothes from the party. His long, dark, shaggy hair was disheveled and sweat-dried. The area below his right eye was slightly swollen. He'd have a nasty black eye in the morning to go along with his hangover from hell. "You should get some ice on that eye."

Jake reached for the bottle, his eyes never leaving her as he twisted off the cap and took a drink. "Thanks for the advice, Dr. Phoenix."

She heavily exhaled as she dropped the bottle of water and Pop-Tart on the couch. "I'll be right back. Going to get you some ice." Not like there wasn't already enough ice in the room.

The bus fired up as she returned with a bag of frozen peas. She caught her balance as the bus lurched forward onto the main road. They'd be in another city in a day, playing another show in front of thousands of screaming fans. The only thing that would make this perfect was if Eli were here experiencing it all. Well, not all of it. Rock and roll was too crazy for a five-year-old, but still, he could meet his favorite rock gods. Jake could meet Eli.

She stopped dead in her tracks. What in the actual fuck was she thinking? Not Jake nor anyone else could know about her son, at least not until after she'd landed the

Gracefall gig. Besides, why did she feel the need to tell Jake about her son?

Because Jake was an amazing guy.

This had to stop, but she couldn't put distance between them. They were stuck together on this bus for the next four months, which had her thinking. There was definitely an attraction between them. Would it hurt to have a little fun? After the tour, they would never see each other again. Friends with benefits with no strings attached. Would Jake go for that?

Usually, that thought would be ridiculous. She didn't need to complicate things further with Dax. But on the other hand, he didn't run her life. He chose to stay away. It was time she moved on and took advantage of the situation. It wasn't like she'd fall in love, but hell, her body was long overdue for some sexual healing.

Elliot straightened her ponytail again, a nervous habit she had. She followed the sound of Jake playing guitar, a lot louder than before. When she walked in, Jake continued to play as if she wasn't there. Guess she was getting the cold shoulder.

"Hey!" she yelled over the shredding strings, which seemed to get even louder. "I couldn't find a bag to put the ice in, so you'll have to settle for frozen peas!"

Jake shook his head. "Can't hear you."

"Frozen peas!" she yelled louder.

God, he was a sight. She'd seen some disturbing rocker things in her life, but this took the cake. A hot rocker dude with nose goblins who looked blasted out of his mind. This was one mental picture she would never forget. Where was her phone?

"Jake!" He ignored her.

"That's it." She reached out and grabbed his guitar, yanking it free from his hands.

"What the fuck?" Jake exclaimed, stunned.

"I'm trying to help you, asshole." She walked out and placed his guitar in its bunk, then returned. "You need ice on that eye." She stood in front of him and was surprised when he let her set the bag on his face. The thick veins in his neck strained as he lay back, resting his head on the back of the couch. "That feels good."

"You know you shouldn't go around picking fights," she teased.

"He started it." Jake sounded like her five-year-old when a kid at the playground took Eli's favorite toy from the sandbox. Eli had hauled off and hit the kid in the face. Needless to say, they weren't welcome in the Mommy and Me Playground Club anymore.

"You both were looking for a fight."

Jake sat up as if he'd just remembered something. "Hey, where's my guitar?"

"Don't worry. I put your precious to bed." She pushed him back and laid the bag of peas on his right eye.

"You know what?"

"Hmm."

"You just popped my guitar cherry."

"Uhh, what?"

"No one else has ever touched that guitar except you."

"Really?"

"I shit you not."

"Well, then I feel honored to have popped your cherry." Her words came out more seductive than she meant.

She removed the tissue from his nose, and he winced. "Sorry. Looks like you've stopped bleeding. Let's clean you up."

She went to the kitchen sink and wet a towel. When she returned, Jake was sitting upright, going for another sip of bourbon.

"I'll take that before you kill yourself." She took the bottle and set it aside, out of reach.

"Elliot, you're a real killjoy. You know that?" His words were slurred.

"No, I just want to see you live another day. That shit will destroy your life." She pushed him back. "Lie back." She straddled him, which was probably a bad idea.

"Hey." He gripped her ass. "I'm down."

She playfully shoved his chest. "Knock it off. I'm cleaning you up. That's it." She wiped the dried blood from the corner of his mouth. His lips were full and oh so kissable. She licked her own lips and swore she could still taste his kiss from this morning.

"You know. I always thought that women liked men to be chivalrous." His hands kneaded her ass, and she allowed it.

"Women like gentlemen. What are you talking about?"

"I saw Dax harassing you. I lost my shit. I couldn't handle him mistreating you."

"I was fine, Jake."

"No, you weren't. The look on your face scared me. I thought Dax was going to hurt you. I wasn't looking for a fight. I just wanted to rescue you."

Elliot paused. Jake was looking out for her? That was an odd reality. Dax never gave a shit about her. It was always about Dax.

"I just thought you would have left the party with me instead of Dax." He grabbed the towel and wiped it under his nose. Even battered and bruised, he still looked sexy.

"It's complicated between Dax and me. We share a lot of history, but that doesn't mean I wasn't concerned about you.

I wanted to make sure you were okay, but I didn't want to piss Dax off."

"Fuck him." He raised his voice and sobered. "He doesn't get to manipulate you like that."

"Jake, you don't understand."

"Then make me, Elliot."

"I can't tell you."

"Right, I'm still the enemy." He threw the towel across the room.

"Stop." She braced her hands on his chest. "You've asked me to trust you, and I'm trying so hard to, but you have to trust me. I can't tell you. The timing isn't right."

He pinned her with the smoldering blue gaze that shot tingles straight to all her girly parts. On their own accord, her hands caressed his pecs. His muscles tightened. "You can trust me with anything, Elliot."

"Good." She smiled. "I was going to talk to you about an arrangement I came up with for us, but seeing as you're blitzed out of your mind, it can wait."

He gripped her ass harder as she tried to move off his lap. "I'm fine. What do you want to talk about? I'm in a truthful mood." A sly grin spread across his lips, and all she could think was *oh shit*.

She cleared her throat. "We should get you to bed. It can wait."

"Nope. Right here, right now. Tell me."

She found herself adjusting her ponytail again. "I think we should fuck."

Jake's eyes widened, and he froze like a deer in headlights. "What? I mean, no question. Yes...yes, we should. When? Like now or—"

Elliot laughed. "Hold up, Pretty Boy. We need to talk about the arrangement first. The rules."

"Rules?"

"Look, we've gone two months on the road living in close quarters. We both know we're not going to make it to the end without fucking. Right?"

"Well, I'd be lying if I said you weren't the lady in my fantasy. The things we do...." he said, losing focus, as if he trailed off into his fantasy.

"Too much information, Jake."

"Sorry. So, what are you suggesting?"

"I'm going to be upfront with you. I'm not the girl you bring home to meet the parents. I'm not the codependent type looking for a relationship or to fall in love. Been there, bought the T-shirt. I like you, Jake. But we both know after the tour we're going our separate ways. So, why not have a little fun?"

"What, Elliot Phoenix wanting to have fun? I dunno."

"Jake, do you or don't you want to fuck me?"

"I feel that's a loaded question."

"Stop joking. I'm serious. Just you and me for the next few months. After the tour, you'll never see me again. Unless I'm in town with the band, and I need a booty call." She winked.

"Oh, you're funny. I think I'll be the one calling for booty."

There was a short silence before Jake answered, leaving Elliot questioning the arrangement. She could handle not falling in love, but could Jake? The last thing she wanted was to hurt him. But this was all she had to give at the moment.

"So, let me get this straight because I'm a rule follower." He cleared his throat. "You and me fucking with no strings attached until the end of the tour?"

Elliot nodded. "And no groupies." She shivered. "You never know where they have been."

"Well, that kinda sounds like a relationship if we're only fucking each other."

"Trust me." She leaned in and kissed his neck. "All you'll need is me."

He laid his head back, allowing her to assault his flesh with hot, wet kisses. Elliot smelled the bourbon on his breath, causing a familiar craving to form in her mouth. She knew better than to even think about having a drink, but the hunger was there. She sat up. "So, what say you, Pretty Boy?"

He shoved his hands in the back of her tank top. "You're not wearing a bra."

"I was going to bed. Stop changing the subject. My offer is about to expire."

He cradled her head with his strong callused hands, causing a shiver to strike down her spine. "I think we're crazy to think we can just say goodbye at the end."

"It's all I can offer, Jake."

"Then, I'll take it."

He drew her to him and claimed her lips. The bourdon she craved fed her greed to deepen the kiss. Their tongues danced to the beginning of their song.

Overwhelmed by the taste of alcohol, Elliot pushed back, breaking the kiss. She wiped her lips as if she'd just taken a drink. "You taste like whiskey."

"Oh shit!" Jake shot off the couch, launching her off to the side. "I'm so sorry!" He grabbed the bourbon bottle and strode to the kitchen, trying to keep his balance in the moving bus. He poured it down the drain, then rinsed his mouth out under the faucet.

Jake returned with a grim expression on his face. He sat down next to her, resting his elbows on his thighs. "If I ever kiss you when I've been drinking, kick me square in the nuts."

"Jake." She took his hand in hers. "It's okay. I'm fine. It was a good reminder to be proud of my five years clean. I can handle it." She gave him a reassuring smile. "Let's go to bed. I'm exhausted, and you need sleep."

She got up and made her way to her bunk. She turned to Jake when he didn't follow her. He'd stopped at his bunk. "What are you doing?"

Puzzled, he looked at her. "Going to bed."

She removed her tank top, giving him a full show of her boobs. "You're sleeping with me."

She watched his Adam's apple bob as he swallowed hard. "Okay."

He tugged his shirt off, fighting with the tee tangling with his cross necklace. She stopped him as he reached for the button of his fly. "Pants on."

"Oh, right." He climbed into the bunk, and Elliot followed. She climbed over him because there was no way she'd spend the night with her ass hanging out of the bunk.

Jake lay on his back with his arm around her as she snuggled close, skin on skin. "Thank you for being my hero tonight." She played with the nipple ring she'd been dying to touch ever since she'd showered with him. That damn thing teased her night after night when Jake went on stage shirtless.

He held her tight. "You're welcome. I'm here to serve and protect." He kissed her forehead.

It wasn't long before Jake passed out.

Elliot laid her head on his chest, listening to him breathe. It felt good being in Jake's arms. He gave her a safety she hadn't realized she'd needed. Had Jake been right? Would she be able to walk away?

11

*J*ake woke with a churning in his stomach and a half-naked Elliot practically lying on top of him. The bunk spun. Fuck. His face throbbed and his ribs moaned as he tried to slip out of bed without waking Elliot. He made it to the bathroom right before last night's booze came up. Jake must have done this five, six times until he was left with dry heaves. He flushed and sat down next to the toilet, resting his throbbing head on the porcelain bowl. Jake had gotten hammered many times, but last night was over the top. He sent a silent promise to whoever was listening that he'd never touch bourbon again.

A knock on the door jolted Jake from sleep. He rubbed his face. Hell, he'd passed out again, waking up on the bathroom floor. "Are you still alive in there?"

He grunted as he sat up. "Yeah." He climbed to his feet and held onto the sink as the bus bounced down the highway, which wasn't helping his current condition. "I'll be out in a minute."

"Okay. Can I make you some breakfast?"

"Oh God, no." Jake turned on the faucet, splashing cool water on his face.

"Are you sure? You should eat something. It will make you feel better."

"Nope." He dried his face off. "I'm good."

The silence was welcoming. Talking made his head feel worse. Jake looked in the mirror. His right eye was swollen, as well as his cheekbone, and dried blood crusted under his nostrils. He took the towel and scrubbed harder until all the blood was gone. He wondered what the other guy looked like.

Jake lifted his arms, examining the stabbing pain on his left side. Yep, a huge bruise had formed over his ribcage. He took another long look in the mirror. Fucking rock and roll.

He still reeked of alcohol, sweat, and...he breathed in profoundly...Elliot. Her fresh coconut lotion or whatever the hell it was invaded his senses, overpowering the other smells. He washed up with a bar of soap and a towel. Hopefully, there was enough deodorant to cover up any residual odors because he was so going to naked cuddle with Elliot again.

Jake walked out of the bathroom feeling like hell warmed over, if that was even a feeling. It was like knocking on death's door, and death wasn't home to ease the pain. Not to mention the bad taste in his mouth.

He sluggishly padded back to the bunks to grab his toothbrush and deodorant when Elliot came up behind him. "Hey."

"Hey." He fumbled around in his bag.

"I made some toast. Plain." She rubbed his shoulder. She really must have felt bad for him.

He turned to face her, and her mouth dropped open.

"Oh. My. God. Jake! Your eye!" She reached over to touch it, but he pulled back.

"It looks worse than it is." Not really. It was so swollen he couldn't see out of it.

"How are you going to play tomorrow night?"

"It'll go down by then, right?" He touched his mammoth-sized shiner.

She stepped in closer, examining it like a mother would do with a child. "I don't know. There's not enough concealer to cover that up. And the swelling." She shook her head. "Fucking Dax."

"I have to admit, he throws a mean right hook."

"I'll see if I can find something to ice your eye."

"Okay. I'm going to brush the death out of my mouth." He waved his toothbrush in the air.

As Jake attended to his oral hygiene, he remembered the arrangement Elliot had brought up. The night had been fuzzy at best, but he completely recalled their conversation. Elliot was in no place for a relationship, or at least that's what she thought. Jake thought differently. He would play along. However, he knew there was a connection between them that wasn't just lust. He really cared for her. If last night didn't prove it, he'd work harder.

Jake finished and headed out into the kitchen, where Elliot, still in boxer shorts and a tank top, was putting a piece of toast on a plate. "Hey." She handed it to him. "Please try to eat."

Jake took the plate, holding back a retch, and sat down at the small kitchen table.

She set down a bottle of Gatorade. "I found it stashed in the fridge."

"Thanks." Jake opened the bottle and took a sip. The

cold orange liquid was refreshing and welcoming; dehydration was a bitch.

Elliot rested her elbows on the table, fidgeting with her fingers.

"Everything okay?" Jake fought against his body, protesting the toast, and took a bite.

"How much do you remember about last night?"

"Most of it. Don't remember how I made it back on the bus, though."

"So, you remember our conversation about..." She pointed to herself, then to him. "Fucking."

Jake's good eye widened. "You want to do it now?"

She shook her head. "No, that's not what I'm getting at."

"I might look like hell, but I'm good to go."

Elliot flashed him a smile. "I bet you are. But no. I was just checking if you remembered."

Did she have buyer's remorse? "You're not going back on the arrangement, are you?"

"No." She shook her head. "I want to make sure you're still cool with it, and it wasn't the bourbon talking."

Jake took another gulp of Gatorade. "I'm willing to go with it. But I should warn you, I'm totally irresistible. Chicks can't keep their hands off me."

Elliot raised her brow playfully. "I'll keep that in mind."

Jake leaned back. "Chicks dig a fighter." He gave her a wicked smile.

She laughed. "Jake, you're full of shit."

"I know. But hey, someone has to stroke my ego."

They smiled at each other. Jake took her in, trying to work up the nerve to ask her out on a date. If that was even possible. He'd rather begin this "fucking agreement" the right way and get to know one another a little more first.

The bus was on schedule, putting them at the venue around five in the evening. Their show was tomorrow night. He had the time, but where to go?

"Hey, you look far away, Pretty Boy."

Jake sat up and went for it. "How about I take you out when we arrive at the venue?"

She crossed her arms over her chest. "Like a date?"

Jake put his hands up in front of him. "Whoa there, cowgirl." He pretended to act surprised. "Date kinda sounds relationship-y. I'm not ready to commit."

"Don't mock me."

"I'm not. Just sticking to the rules. How about two friends hanging out with an option for fucking?"

Elliot eyed him a second before responding. "It'd be nice to get off this bus for a while." She paused. "Okay. Where are we going?"

"Not sure. What's your favorite food?"

"I'd do anything for some Italian."

"I'll do what I can."

～

The bus had pulled into the venue right on time. After a nap, a river of water, and Advil, Jake felt like a new man, except for the massive shiner on his right eye.

"Be still," Elliot huffed as she dabbed concealer under his eye.

"Woman, it hurts." The swelling had gone down, and he could open his eye, but the motherfucker throbbed like a heartbeat.

"Well, you shouldn't go around hitting people," Elliot smirked, and it was the cutest thing he'd ever seen.

Elliot was dressed in a black tank top with "Be Humble" written in bold white letters on the front, a denim jacket, and black jeans that snugged her body perfectly. Her heavy black stage makeup was gone and replaced with natural, glowing color. She'd even curled her hair. Not that he was checking her out.

Elliot stepped back, inspecting her work. "You might want to wear sunglasses. There's not enough concealer in the world to hide that shiner."

Jake looked in the mirror. "It's much better than it was, but we should both wear our shades, just in case someone recognizes us."

"Good call. So, where are you taking me?" Elliot asked as she searched the counter for her sunglasses.

"It's a surprise."

"You should know I don't like surprises."

He could have guessed that. The slightest change-up in routine, and you would think the sky was falling. "Yep, I figured that one out fast."

"What's that supposed to mean?" She put her hands on her hips.

"I've noticed how much you like routine."

"Routine is good."

"Sure, it is," he said with more mockery than intended. "That's why the other day you lost your shit when the bus driver had to take a detour."

"I just wanted to know what was going on."

"But it's borderline OCD when you whip out the road map and dictate to the driver where he should be going when it had been clear he knew what he was doing."

Elliot shrugged. "I see no harm in using a map instead of relying on an app. Besides, it's perfectly healthy to double-check the routes."

"Right."

A text message alert rang from Jake's cell, lying on the kitchen table. He picked it up. "Looks like our ride is here."

Elliot looked out the front window. "A limo, Jake? You got a limo?"

"Yep. Cashed in a rock star perk." He winked and held the bus door open for her. He wasn't about to tell her he'd called Cherry to set up the limo.

Elliot stopped next to him. "I'm impressed." She kissed him on the cheek, then walked off the bus.

Holding back a smile was impossible when he saw how happy Elliot was as the limo parked outside of an Italian restaurant. The surrounding area was a quaint, lowkey downtown area just off the water. He'd heard how beautiful Florida beaches were and wanted to share this experience with Elliot.

"I can't believe you pulled this off, Jake."

"I hope the food is good. It's a five-star restaurant."

The driver opened the door for them. Elliot got out first and waited for him on the curb. He took in the awe on her face as she observed the storefronts next to the restaurant. Elliot deserved to be wined and dined. He couldn't imagine Dax doing something like this for her.

They walked into the restaurant; garlic and Italian seasonings immediately flooded his senses, causing his stomach to roll. Hangovers were a bitch.

No one recognized them as they were led by a petite hostess, who sat them in a circular booth in a private corner. Italian music played softly in the background as he watched Elliot check out the menu. Everything about her was beautiful and intriguing, from the way she tucked her hair behind her ear to the way she innocently sucked in her bottom lip as she decided on her meal. He could watch her forever.

She placed the menu down and looked confused. "Are you going to look at the menu?"

"Think I'm going to stick with the breadsticks and water."

"Jake, we didn't have to go out if you weren't feeling well."

"I'm fine, and I wanted to take you out. Seeing you happy and enjoying yourself is all I need." He slid closer, resting his arm on the back of the booth as she snuggled against him, fitting perfectly. "Have I told you that you look incredibly sexy tonight?"

She turned and faced him. Her blue catlike eyes soft and playful. "No, but your eyes have." She reached over and fidgeted with the cross around his neck. "You're pretty hot yourself."

"Hot?"

She pressed her lips together and nodded as she eyed him up and down like she wanted to devour him. Hell yeah, he'd take that.

"So, if I'm hot, how do I enter sexy status?"

"Well, it definitely helps to have a sexy chick sitting next to you."

"So, I'm halfway there?"

"Oh, for sure," she teased.

They were so close, and the moment was right, so Jake went in for the kill. He caressed her cheek before drawing her into a soft, gentle kiss. He slid his tongue past her lips to connect with hers. Their tongues explored each other with comfortable ease, like they were made for kissing.

Her hand slipped through his hair as she deepened the

kiss. It felt good knowing she wanted him just as bad as he wanted her, if that was even possible.

A woman cleared her throat. "Can I take your order?" She sounded agitated by the scene, but Jake didn't care. He was kissing his dream girl.

Elliot pulled away, wiping her mouth and straightening in her seat. "Umm, yes. I'll have the eggplant parmesan and a side salad. Thank you." She handed the waitress her menu.

"And for you, sir?"

"Oh, no thanks. Just keep the water and garlic knots coming."

She grabbed the menu off the table and left as quickly as she came.

Jake went to continue where they left off when Elliot changed directions. "So, how are you liking being on the road?"

Deflated, he sat back, still resting his arm behind her on the booth. The way she pulled back led him to believe she was nervous about being out on a date. "Feels like a wild rollercoaster ride. Like we just left Cali."

"Yeah, it's crazy how fast time flies, yet boredom still kicks in."

"There's a lot of downtime on the bus. Though I'm glad we're bus mates. I like that we can just hang and jam, you know?"

"Yeah." She smiled. "Me too. Who would have thought that enemies could be friends?"

"Just for the record, I never considered you an enemy."

A while later, the waitress returned with Elliot's dinner and a fresh basket of garlic knots. Throughout dinner, they talked about the shows and which venues had been their favorite. For Jake, hands down, it was the Dallas Cowboys

Cheerleaders shower escapade. Fucking Texas was incredible. Elliot kept the conversation short when the topic of family came up. She'd come from a long line of nurses. Her grandmother, mother, and sister were nurses. Her mother was retired but still volunteered at the local hospital where her sister, Sarah, currently worked. He learned that they all lived in Nevada and were close.

It was nice to finally get to know about her family. He felt Elliot was trusting him more, which must have been a big step forward for her.

Elliot pushed away her half-eaten plate. "Oh. My. God. Why did you let me eat all that?"

"I wasn't about to come between you and that eggplant. I'm glad you enjoyed it."

"Very much so. And the company was good, too."

He went in for another kiss, but she stopped him. Her hand flew over her mouth. "Jake, I just ate a ton of garlic. You can't possibly want to kiss me."

"So? Me too." He scooted in closer. "I can kiss other parts of you." He tucked her hair off to the side and nuzzled her neck, laying kisses just below her ear. "Elliot, I could kiss you all day long if you'd let me."

She leaned her head to the side, obviously enjoying his kisses. "I'd definitely let you."

He pushed her jean jacket off her shoulder just enough so he could kiss it. Her coconut scent drove him crazy with need. Jake didn't care that they were in a restaurant and people could see what he was doing. He was alone with Elliot, and that's all that mattered.

Her sweet moans were like a kickass, dirty guitar riff that made you want to fuck. Her hands slipped under his shirt, and Jake almost lost his shit. "You need a breath mint so I can kiss you."

She laughed.

He'd never wanted a woman like he wanted Elliot right now. Slowly, he tugged the front of her shirt from her jeans and worked his way up under her bra. He palmed a breast. His thumb moved over her tight nipple, causing her to moan his name.

Jake squeezed her breast, which fit perfectly in his hand. "I love when you say my name." He kissed her earlobe.

"There's something I need to do," she said breathlessly.

"If that thing you need to do is me right here, right now, then game on."

She playful shoved him away. "No. But you do make it hard for a girl to say no."

Jake straightened in his seat, trying to relieve his throbbing dick. No way would they get away with having sex at the restaurant. Besides, they had all night. No need to rush. He just needed a minute until his dick got the message. "So, what is it?"

A wicked smirk stretched across her lips. "You'll see."

Jake barely had time to pay for dinner before Elliot rushed out the door. He'd just stepped outside as she darted across the street. "Hey, hold up," he called after her as he waited for a car to pass by.

He caught up with her as she stood in front of a tattoo shop. Through the window, she watched a guy getting a tattoo. "I've been waiting to do this for a long time."

Jake followed her gaze inside the shop. He was tattooless, and he couldn't recall if Elliot had any. If she did, it had been well hidden. "You want to get a tattoo?" He turned his gaze back to her, but she was already inside.

Jake followed, and heavy metal music played in tune with the buzzing sound of tattoo machines. Artwork littered the walls, which he assumed was by the tattoo artists at the shop. A heavily tattooed guy sitting behind the counter ignored them, swiping across the screen of his phone, wholly lost in cell phone zombie land. Perhaps they were interrupting his break.

"Are you sure you want to do this?" Jake asked Elliot as she flipped through a portfolio of artwork.

"Jake, yes. I have to."

"Okay."

Their conversation alerted the guy behind the counter, and he looked up from his phone. "Holy shit!"

Jake and Elliot froze.

"Gracefall. You guys are from Gracefall. I fucking love you guys."

Elliot approached the man with a smile. "Can you do me a favor?"

"Anything," he said in awe.

Elliot took off her jacket and gave it to Jake. She removed her shirt and turned her back to the guy. "Get rid of this." She pointed to her right upper shoulder.

The tattoo artist leaned over the counter the same time Jake examined her not-so-hidden tattoo. How in the hell had he missed that?

"Wow! That is one faded, jacked-up tatt, sweetheart. Who's Dax?" the guy asked.

"A bad mistake." She turned back around, and Jake refrained from covering her with her jacket.

Now everything made sense. Elliot wanted to erase Dax from her body.

"Tonight has been slow, so you're in luck," the tattooist said. "Besides, you're Elliot fucking Phoenix. My chair is your throne."

"Hold on," Jake interrupted. "Elliot, I'm all for you

covering up your tattoo, but do you know anything about this guy's work. Like, is he legit?"

The man folded as if Jake's words had insulted him. Jake sized the guy up. The dude's arms were thick as tree trunks and covered in tattoos. Yeah, he wasn't looking for a fight. He hadn't recovered from his last one. "No offense."

The guy tipped his chin toward a wall of framed certificates. "None taken."

There were several awards, a picture of the dude with the hosts and judges of a famous tattoo competition television show, and a plethora of certificates of expertise. He turned to Elliot. "So, what are you having done?"

"I want something unique. Something that represents me and new beginnings." She faced Jake. "What do you think?"

The tattoo artist began giving her his recommendations, but by the look on Elliot's face, she wasn't feeling it.

Jake had an idea. He ripped the sign-in page out of the binder, flipped it over to the clean side, and began drawing. Within minutes he'd had a rough sketch to show Elliot.

"How about something like this?" He handed the drawing to Elliot. Her eyes widened and became watery. Shit, he didn't mean to make her cry. "I thought a phoenix rising from flames above a pile of ash was a good representation of you. Your past is the ash, and the phoenix rising is your future. I didn't mean to upset you."

"Jake!" She threw her arms around his neck, squeezing him tight. "I love it. It's exactly me." She let him go. "I had no idea your talents went beyond playing guitar. What other talents are you keeping from me, Pretty Boy?"

Jake couldn't hold back the sly grin from forming on his lips. "Well—"

"How about we get this design on paper." The tattoo

artist changed the subject as he rubbed his hands together, not interested in Jake's other talents.

To say seeing her this excited was the best day of his life would be an understatement. No longer would she be reminded of her past. She deserved happiness and to be free from Dax on her skin.

ive hours later and Elliot was finally free from the hideous tattoo on her skin. Now, she had a gorgeous, fiery phoenix on her shoulder. And best of all, Jake had designed it. No one had ever done something like this for her. As she looked in the mirror at the shop, she realized just how much Jake knew her.

"That's fucking amazing, dude," Jake said to the tattoo artist. "Elliot, look at the ashes. You can't see Dax's name at all."

Elliot smiled, for she had no words.

She went to pay the artist, and he raised his hand, stopping her. "Anything for Gracefall. Besides, that smile on your face is enough for me. I'm glad I could help."

Elliot was beyond grateful. The whole night had to have been a dream. She'd wake up any moment back on the bus, traveling to the next gig with the same old Dax tattoo and Jake on her mind. "I can't thank you enough." She hugged the artist.

"Any time you or the rest of the crew are in town, stop in. Tell them to come see Dave."

"That's a deal."

"We should be heading out," Jake said. "Dave, you're one awesome dude." They shoulder bumped.

Elliot got into the limo, still high on getting new ink. She couldn't wait to show Eli and Sarah. Hell, she wanted to show the whole world.

"I'm really proud of you, Elliot." Jake sat next to her, handing her a bottle of water from the small wet bar.

"Thanks." She grinned, suddenly feeling shy. "I've wanted to do this for a long time. And since I'm breaking a lot of rules lately, might as well break one more."

Ever since she'd met Jake, she'd been breaking her rules, especially rule number one to never get involved with a rock star. But Jake wasn't really a rock star. He was different, which made him intriguing and dangerous. She wasn't supposed to fall for the enemy. Jake was to be defeated. Nothing could interfere with landing the Grace-fall gig and bringing Eli on the road with her so they could be a family.

"You had a rule about getting tattoos?"

She rolled her eyes. "Obviously, you saw my mistake."

"True. But I think you're in a better place now. You should trust yourself more." He held her hand. "You deserve happiness."

She looked at their interlocked fingers as Jake rubbed his thumb across the top of her hand. "You're right, but it's complicated." Right there, on the tip of her tongue, she wanted to tell Jake about her son but couldn't risk it, which tore at her heart. He'd never lied to her. He was in her corner, making her feel like she was a better person. Why couldn't she let her guard down?

"Jake, I need to tell you something."

"Sure."

"Where to?" The limo driver interrupted just in time before she spilled her guts. What was she thinking?

"Back to the bus?" Jake asked. "Unless you want to go somewhere else."

"The bus is good. I'm a little tired."

"To the bus," Jake answered the chauffeur, then closed the divider between them and the driver. He turned in his seat and faced her. "What do you need to tell me?"

His deep-blue eyes narrowed in on hers. He looked curious and seemed intrigued.

Fuck!

"I just wanted to thank you for a beautiful night."

Coward! Total copout. Inside, she cringed.

Jake didn't need to know about Eli. Another brick laid around her heart. She'd do anything for her son, even if it meant suppressing her own happiness.

Jake gazed deeply into her eyes, and for a moment, she swore he saw through the lie. "I'm glad you enjoyed yourself. I'd like to do it again."

"Hmm. That kinda sounds like a relationship blooming. Not sure if that's part of our arrangement," she teased, taking the focus off of her.

Jake leaned back into the seat, resting his hands behind his head, and sighed. "You're probably right."

"Breach of contract could hold heavy consequences." Elliot set the water bottle down then straddled Jake, catching him off guard.

His hands slid around to her ass and squeezed. "Like what?"

"Sexual frustration." She pulled Jake's T-shirt off, then ran her hands down the hills and valleys of his abdomen.

"That's a hefty penalty."

She nodded, seductively biting her bottom lip. "So, Mr.

Police Officer, are you going to uphold your oath to the fullest?"

"Well, ma'am, it's my moral duty to serve and protect." Jake flashed a crooked, sexy grin that sent a shiver streaking down her spine. He slipped his hands up the back of her shirt, releasing her from her bra.

Elliot snaked her hands behind his neck. She was sure her pirate-like grin was giving herself away to the fantasy playing in her head as she bent down and kissed him hard. Not wanting to wait, she slipped her tongue past his lips, allowing Jake to take over all her senses.

There was no more thinking, only letting her body react to Jake. It was only sex, she reminded herself.

She pulled back long enough to remove her tank top and bra. Jake's gaze settled on her breasts as he palmed one in each hand. "You're fucking beautiful, Elle." He leaned in and took her nipple into his mouth. The roughness of his beard teased her tight nipple and sent another shiver through her. He knew exactly where she wanted to be kissed.

He moved over to her other breast and lapped her other nipple, giving it the same attention as he had the other. She leaned her head back, marveling at the wicked sensations Jake was giving her body.

She hadn't been with anyone else since Dax. It was definitely time to enjoy herself, and she was relishing Jake's mouth on her. "Jake."

"Yeah, baby," he murmured in between kisses and licks.

"I so fucking need you right now." She thrust her hips forward, grinding on his hardened cock.

Jake stopped and looked up at her. He brushed the hair back from her face. "Elle, are you sure? In the limo?"

Elliot nodded and bit her bottom lip like a naughty

schoolgirl. She popped open the button on his jeans, then unzipped him. She reached inside and took his cock in her hand. "I need you, Jake."

She stroked him and kissed his neck, letting him know she was serious. He felt good in her hands, and he'd feel even better inside her.

As if he read her mind, he lifted her up and set her down beside him. He yanked his jeans down as Elliot worked on her own, kicking off her heels and unbuttoning her pants. She couldn't get them off fast enough.

Elliot couldn't wait any longer for Jake to unlace his boots to get his jeans off, so she straddled him, practically attacking him. He wrapped his arms around her waist and pulled her against him. The feel of his hot, sweaty skin on hers set her insides to flames. She'd never wanted someone as much as she wanted Jake right now.

She reached between them, stroking him against her sex, getting used to the feel of his cock.

"Elle, you're so fucking wet." He kissed her neck.

"It's your fault," she whispered next to his ear as she stroked him over her swollen clit.

He was big and long. Elliot worried if she would be able to take him all in. Not to mention the pain she'd endure since it had been three years since she had sex. But she didn't care. Whatever the pain, it was worth every ache to feel alive again.

She heard the wrinkling of a wrapper being torn open behind her. Jake rolled the condom on himself.

"You always come prepared?"

"Well, I am under contract, right? Have to be prepared." He winked.

She lifted, then slowly lowered herself over the tip of his cock. Every sweet inch of him filling her, stretching her, stung and awakened a beautiful sensation she hadn't felt in a long time.

To her surprise, she took all of him in like they were made to fit perfectly together. He gripped her ass. "Fuck me, you feel amazing." Jake hissed.

"We feel fucking amazing together." She bent down and claimed his lips as she pulled back, then slid back down his dick again faster than the first time.

The sensation between her legs demanded more. The pain quickly subsided, and she thrust her hips back and forth, taking everything Jake was giving.

It wasn't long before she was racing toward the edge of shattering. One right move from Jake would be her undoing.

He slipped his hand between them, stroking her clit with his fingers. "Jake." His hands played her to perfection like a flawless guitar solo. She whimpered into his neck as she rode the lightning bolt streaking through her body. "I'm going to come."

"Let it go, Elle. I got you."

It was as though he'd commanded her body to release because she did just that. The wave came fast and hard, causing her to feel weightless. She tightened her legs around Jake, trying to stop her body from quivering, but it was useless. Her orgasm rocked her to the core. Jake had rocked her to the core.

As she recovered, he wrapped his arms around her, holding her. Being in his arms was magic. His warmth took all her worries away. She lifted her head and noticed a bite mark on his shoulder. She hadn't realized she had bitten him. "Jake, I'm so sorry."

"What?" He looked at his shoulder, then wickedly grinned at her. "Totally worth it." He held her head, one hand on each side of her face, and caressed her cheek. "I have never seen a more beautiful moment than watching you come." The air in her lungs seized, and a lump formed in her throat. Shit, was she going to cry?

He drew her in and kissed her softly.

"Limo sex. Check that off the bucket list," he joked, turning the lump in her throat to laughter. She didn't know how he did it, but he always knew when to lighten her mood.

She climbed off him and began putting on her jeans and tank top as Jake cleaned up, disposing of the condom.

Jake sat down next to her as he finished putting on his jeans. They sat in awkward silence. She didn't know what to say. With Dax, sex had always been awkward afterward. He'd be coked out of his head most of the time, unable to satisfy her. The only time she'd brought it up, he'd gotten pissed off and didn't talk to her for a week.

"Hey." Jake held her hand to his lips and kissed it. "What's going on in that pretty little head of yours?"

She shrugged. "The problem is nothing is wrong."

"I don't understand. Is there supposed to be something wrong? Because I can't find anything wrong with what just happened."

"No, it was perfect." She took in a deep breath. "I'm not used to perfect, Jake. I was high most of the time when Dax and I had sex, and he was the last guy I slept with."

He put his arm around her, and she snuggled next to him. "Well, I can make you one promise, Elle. Sex with me will always be satisfying, or else we'll keep trying until it is. And I'll never be on drugs."

"That was two promises."

"Yeah, well, I'm feeling generous."

Elliot ran her fingers up and down his arm as she built up the nerve to ask him a question. "Are you going to

Melody and Joe's engagement party next weekend at Leo Sterling's LA home?"

"Yeah. How about you?"

"Yes. Are you staying for the whole weekend?" Melody had invited the band to stay the weekend at her dad's house. Joe and Dylan had been secretly working on a song for Melody and wanted the band to play it for her at the engagement party. Elliot loved the idea and maybe was a tad bit jealous.

"Yeah. I can't wait to see the God of Thunder's estate. I bet it's amazing."

"Cool." She picked at a piece of lint on her jeans, procrastinating.

"Elle, you have something you want to say?"

That's it. Jake was officially a mind reader. "Yeah, I thought since you'll be there, and I'll be there that we could...you know—"

"Go together?"

"I mean, we'll both be there. Might as well."

"Of course." He shrugged one shoulder. "It makes total sense."

"Cool." She smiled up at him, relieved to have finally got it all out without sounding like a stuttering mess.

Jake caressed her cheek and looked deeply into her eyes. Her heart skidded to a halt. "Elle."

God, she loved the way her new nickname rolled off his tongue.

"I know you don't want a relationship. I get that. But there isn't anyone else I want to be with." His thumb brushed over her bottom lip.

Elliot didn't know what to say. She liked Jake a lot, but she wasn't about to break another rule. Absolutely no relationships. "Jake." She shook her head. "Don't do this. Let's just live in the moment."

"I know. I just wanted to tell you." He kissed the top of her head. "Jeez, Elle, no need to get all needy. Seriously, give a man space," he joked again, making her chuckle.

13

The pool was as gorgeous as the inside of Leo Sterling's Mediterranean-style mansion. It was like a lazy river that snaked through his backyard, with a huge rock waterfall that created a dramatic wall in one corner of the pool. Palm trees and various tropical plants were strategically spread out through the area, providing privacy and giving off an island vibe. It was like a vacation.

Elliot lay in a chaise lounge chair, which had the most comfortable cushions ever, under a beautiful California mid-day November sun. But the best part yet, no boys.

She was enjoying time with Melody, Dani, and Cherry, which was unusual for her. Jill, her manager, had been her only friend in recent years besides her sister. So, having some girl time felt great.

Since Dani was best friends with Melody, Elliot had seen a lot of her on tour, mostly hanging around Dylan. Elliot loved Cherry. She was a crazy chick, and they had hit it off right from the start. And then there was Melody, rock and roll royalty. To say she was a little intimidated being in presence of the God of Thunder's daughter was an understatement. Even though Mel was sweet, Elliot still felt out of place.

"Oh. My. God!" Melody exclaimed as she watched a video on her cell. "I'm totally having one of these at my wedding." She turned her phone so everyone could see the video.

Elliot lifted her aviators and watched a happy guy dancing down the aisle, tossing rose petals.

Dani busted out laughing. "Why do I see Tyler doing this?"

"Yes!" Melody beamed. "He's doing this. I just need to talk Joe into having a flower dude instead of a flower girl."

"Good luck there," Cherry added as she lay back down. Her pale-pink hair matched her halter-top bikini. Elliot might need to call an intervention; the girl was obsessed with pink.

"I have my ways," Melody grinned.

"Ugh!" Dani huffed. "You guys are sickening. Cute, but sickening."

"Don't be jealous. You know how it is with those Grace brothers."

Elliot turned her head toward Dani. "I didn't know you and Dylan were a thing."

"We're not." Dani fidgeted with the mass of dark hair pulled up high on her head.

"Booty call," Melody corrected. "She's Dylan's booty call."

"Shut up," Dani spat back.

"Hey, there's nothing wrong with that," Elliot added. "I've seen a lot being on the road with rock stars. As long as you know where you stand, you won't get hurt."

"No, you'll just end up with crabs or some other sexually transmitted disease." Cherry laughed. "I'm swatting chicks left and right, trying to keep them away from the guys. Dylan loves his groupies."

Dani shrugged. "He's free to have sex with whoever he wants. I'm free to do my thing."

"Um, Elliot, I think you should see this." A horrified look washed over Melody's face.

Elliot sat up. "What?" Melody handed her the phone. Her heart dropped as she saw a picture of her and Jake making out in the Italian restaurant he'd taken her to. "Shit!"

Cherry bounced up, swiping the phone from Elliot. "You and Jake are a thing?"

"It was nothing." Elliot tried to play it off, but being outed on social media was freaking her out. This wasn't the way she wanted her bandmates to find out, and now her chances of getting the gig were at risk. Not to mention what Dax would do when he found out. Her heart raced. What was she going to do?

Melody took her phone back. "Well, I think it's great. You guys have amazing chemistry on stage. It's no wonder you two are together."

"No, Melody, this isn't good. The guys won't like this."

"Look, I've known Joe, Dylan, and Tyler for a long time, way before they became famous. Tyler won't care. Dylan will high-five ya and give you his typical 'Fuck yeah, dude.' And Joe, I'll talk to him. Everything will be fine." Melody gave her a reassuring smile. Elliot wished she could believe her, but something inside warned her that this situation was far from over.

"Done," Cherry announced as she put her phone down. "I just texted Kimmy. She'll have that picture off all social media in an hour like nothing ever happened."

"Are you sure?" There was no way that Kimmy had some

magic wand to wave over the situation and make it disappear. No one was that lucky. Well, maybe if you had a fancy lawyer. They were like magical fairy godmothers.

"Positive." Cherry tucked her pink hair over to one shoulder as she lay back onto the lounge, sipping a fruity pink cocktail. "That's why Kimmy gets paid the big bucks. I need to ask for a raise. Babysitting rock stars on the road is exhausting."

"Yeah, it is." Melody snorted. "Dylan about killed me."

Melody had been the band's tour manager over the summer. Joe and Melody had a history; they had been best friends since they were kids. But what had pulled on her heartstrings was the way Leo Sterling had taken Joe under his wing and taught him everything he knew about drumming, which led to the birth of Gracefall. Having that kind of support is huge. "Mel, I heard you had to handcuff him to the bed because he was wasted and out of control."

"Yep. Not one of my proudest moments, but at least Dylan didn't end up in jail."

Cherry leaned over and reached into her bag, pulling out a pair of pink fuzzy handcuffs. She tossed them to Elliot. "Never leave home without them." They laughed.

"Hey, ladies," Dylan sang as he, Joe, Tyler, and Jake walked toward them. It was mid-day, and Dylan already had a bottle of whiskey in hand. "Chicks in bikinis. Fuck yeah, dude."

Joe walked past him, shaking his head to Melody. He bent down, cupped the back of her neck, and kissed her passionately. "Hey, sunbathing beauty."

She looked up at him, glowing in love. Elliot wondered if she looked like that when she set eyes on Jake. "You come to crash the party, Rock Star?"

"Yep. But first, your shoulders are getting red. Where's the sunscreen?"

Dani tossed a bottle of SPF 50 to Joe. He sat down behind Melody, straddling her with his big tree-trunk legs, and applied sunscreen on her shoulders and back. "You should be more responsible, Mel. Skin cancer is extremely dangerous."

Melody shook her head. "Hanging around rock stars is dangerous."

Dylan took up residence on Dani's lounge chair, resting his head between her legs. "Daani," he pleaded as he slid a finger under her bikini top. "Tell me you love me. I need to feel loved."

Dani gazed down at Dylan, biting her bottom lip and squirming sensually underneath him.

"Oh, for fuck's sake." Tyler huffed, tossing his towel on a nearby table. "You all need a room." He ran toward the pool. "Cannonball!" He jumped in, causing a tsunami of a wave and splashing everyone. As Tyler emerged from the water, he shook his head like a dog and said, "What's up, mother-fuckahs!"

Cherry shrieked as the cold water hit her. "Asshole!" She shot out of the lounge chair and jumped in after him.

Joe picked up Melody and walked toward the pool. "Ladies first." He tossed her in before she had time to protest.

"Fuck yeah, dude!" Dylan jumped in, joining the tempest of splashing and dunking.

Jake looked at Elliot with a sly grin. "Oh no, you don't," Elliot opposed. "My tattoo is still healing."

He sat down beside her. "Let me have a look."

Elliot tilted forward. "Don't need a bandage anymore, but I'm staying out of the pool."

He inspected the phoenix on her shoulder. "Looks great."

"Daani," Dylan interrupted as he hung on the side of the pool, trying to get Dani's attention. "Is horny an emotion? Because I'm feeling very emotional right now."

"Go away." Dani ignored the question.

"I need you. Like reeeally need you." He scrubbed a hand down his face, wiping the water away. His long, blond mohawk hung in his face, dripping wet.

"You're too needy." Dani shot him a perturbed grin.

Elliot totally understood why women were attracted to Dylan. He reeked of bad boy sex appeal with his lean and toned body. His chest and arms were covered in ink. She almost felt sorry for Dani, who was probably defenseless against that smoldering gaze of his.

"Dani, come play with me," Dylan begged. "Promise I'll bite."

"Dylan Grace," Dani shot him a glare. "You're unbelievable sometimes, you know that?"

"What? I'm totally believable. I'm a golden god. Now get off your high horse and come play with me, woman."

"Dani," Elliot said in her kindest, most patient voice. "For the love of God, make him stop before I kill him."

Dani rolled her eyes as she stood. "He always gets what he wants."

"We're rock stars." Elliot sat back, relaxing in her chair.

"Don't I know it." Dani sauntered off to the pool.

Elliot turned her attention back on Jake. She swallowed hard, trying to get past him looking like a golden god himself. The sun had brought out the lighter highlights in his shaggy brown hair. A soft sheen of sweat glistened over his muscular chest. Her hands itched to journey down the trail of wetness running down his abdomen and disappearing into the waistband of his swim trunks.

Jake took over Cherry's lounge chair, which sat next to Elliot. Through her sunglasses, she kept her eyes on Jake. He took her breath away as he eye-fucked her with his vibrant blue smolder. God help her. The man was indeed something else. "I like your suit."

She didn't need her hormones going off like the Fourth of July. They had bigger issues. "Jake, we need to talk."

He put his hands behind his head. "What's up?"

"Did you see the picture of us on social media?"

"Yes, I did." He grinned and wiggled his brows.

"Why didn't you text me as soon as you saw?" She shoved his leg. "Jake, this is serious."

"I'm glad you feel the same way. I'm glad we're having this discussion because I think it's time to renegotiate our arrangement. At least the relationship part."

"That's not what I'm talking about. This could ruin our chance to land this gig. Well, at least one of us. Did the guys say anything to you?"

"No."

"Are they acting strange?"

Jake flashed her an are-you-serious glare.

"You know what I mean."

"Tyler high-fived me right before we came out here."

"Shit, they know," she exhaled.

"Elle, I don't understand why you're upset over this. The guys haven't said a word. Besides, they don't care."

"I hope you're right." Elliot couldn't tell him that she worried about Dax finding out, because then she would have to explain Eli, and she wasn't ready for that. "Cherry said Kimmy was doing damage control."

"See." He bumped her leg with his. "Nothing to worry about."

Her phone vibrated on the table next to them. She picked it up.

Sarah?

"Jake, I have to take this."

He gave her a chin up, then closed his eyes, taking in the sun.

"Hey." Elliot walked over to the pool cabana for privacy. "How's Eli?" She sat down on the cream-colored cushions, praying everything was okay. But an unexpected call from her sister pulled her insides taut.

"Eli is fine. He's with mom, shopping. That's not why I called."

"Okay, then what?"

"When were you going to tell me that Dax has visitation rights now?"

"He doesn't."

"Then why was he here demanding to see Eli?"

Ice plagued her body, freezing her to the core. She couldn't breathe. What was Dax doing at her sister's place? Why did he want to see Eli?

Oh. My. God.

"Elliot, talk to me. Are you okay?" Sarah asked, probably panicked by Elliot's lack of response.

"Yeah, give me a second." Elliot took in a couple deep breaths. Eli was with her mom; he was safe.

"What's going on, E?"

"Dax has been calling me. I warned him to stay away. I never gave him permission to see Eli. We've discussed nothing of the sort." God, she couldn't breathe.

"E, calm down. Nothing is going to happen to Eli. He's safe, okay?"

"I can't believe the bastard had the nerve to try and see him. What if Eli was home? Oh, God!" Elliot stood and paced the length of the patio couch. "I'm coming home. I'm in LA. I can be there tonight if I leave right now."

"You're freaking out, sis. You don't need to race over here. I got this. When mom comes back, we'll head to her place. Dax won't find us there."

"No, I really think I should be there."

"No, you don't. The whole reason Eli is staying with me is so you can land this gig. Don't jeopardize it by coming home just yet. Eli is fine. I'll have him FaceTime you later tonight, yes?"

"Of course!" Her voice cracked on the verge of crying. "I miss him." Elliot's eyes teared up.

"Hey, don't worry. I can handle Dax Gage."

At least someone could. "In the meantime, I'll call Dax." Avoiding his calls hadn't been wise. He was making it known that he wasn't to be ignored.

"Not to change the subject, but I was on social media this morning. When were you going to tell me about Jake Quin?"

Fuck!

"There's nothing to tell, Sarah. He's a good friend."

"Making out in public sounds like more than friends. Elliot, he's freaking hot!"

Elliot was surprised when she smiled at her sister's comment. "Seriously, it's nothing. It's probably why Dax showed up at the house. Jake punched Dax for getting out of line the other night after a show. I should have talked to Dax then, but I didn't."

"Jake defending your honor? So, when are you bringing him home so we can meet him? You know mom will want to have him over for dinner."

"I don't know. I haven't told Jake about Eli yet. I'm not sure it's a good idea right now. We're fighting for the same gig. I can't give him anything that he could use against me."

"You actually think he would do that?"

Deep down, Elliot knew Jake wasn't deceiving. She just had a hard time trusting her instincts when it came to men. "Sarah," Elliot huffed. "I just don't know anymore. I'm tired of lying to everyone about Eli." But mostly, she was tired of hating Dax. It took up too much energy. And pretending he was dead wasn't working either.

"I know. I wish I had better advice for you, but I'm afraid we're cursed when it comes to men." Her older sister had finalized her third divorce in three years. Sarah was right; the Phoenix girls fell fast and hard in love. It's why Elliot had stayed so guarded. Even now, after what Dax had done to her, she felt herself slip back into her old ways, wanting to find the good in him. To hold onto that goodness and pretend everything could work out.

Elliot took in a deep breath. She was losing focus.

"I think you should talk to Jake. You looked incredibly happy with him. Happier than I've seen you."

"Yeah, I don't know, sis. I really don't want to talk about Jake anymore. I'll see ya tonight on FaceTime. Can't wait to talk to Eli."

"You bet. Talk soon."

Elliot hung up, shutting that shit down fast. Jake wasn't a topic she wanted to discuss, especially with her sister. It was only sex. Nothing complicated about that.

Her gaze fell onto Jake, basking under the rays. Taking him inside up to her room and running her hands over his bronze skin sounded a lot better than dealing with her ex. In the short time they had known each other, he'd turned her inside out. She was no longer emotionally numb. She was happy.

Realization slammed into her. *Happy?*

Elliot had been happily in love once. Being on cloud nine for a time had been nice. But the thing about love is that it fucks with your brain. It's cunning and blinding. And oh, how she'd been blinded by Dax. Love is complicated, disguised in beauty that fades into a beast.

Then along came Jake, changing her mind about everything in her life. She'd tried to believe in love. Really, she had. With Jake, it would be so easy. She loved his humor and the way her stomach flipped like an Olympic diver every time he walked into the room. There was something so comforting in the way he looked at her.

But wanting and needing something were two different demons of their own. Elliot didn't want to believe in Jake; she needed to.

Analyzing the situation to the point of confusion and irritation, Elliot decided to tackle the Dax issue. She found Dax's last text message and started a new one.

Elliot: We need to talk. NOW!

She waited for what seemed like forever for Dax to respond. A gray blinking text bubble appeared.

Dax: Heading back from Reno. Will be in LA in three hours. Meet me at my place?

Elliot: I'll be there.

Dax: Head over anytime. You know where the key is.

God, even in his text messages, the guy was a cocky bastard. Elliot didn't respond further.

With her mood now in pissed-off mode, because dealing with Dax would do that to a girl, she took in a deep breath and walked over to Jake. "Hey, I have something I have to take care of. I'll be back late tonight." She could hope, as long as she didn't end up in prison for murder. Already, she felt the hate bubbling in her veins. Note to self, keep away from all sharp objects that could potentially become lethal projectiles.

Without waiting for his response, she headed toward the house.

"Wait." Jake sat up, lowering his Aviators. "Hold up."

Elliot paused because, of course, it was Jake. She turned around, irritated he'd stopped her. "What?"

"Where are you going?"

"It's none of your business, Jake. I'll be back tonight, okay?"

"No, it's not okay." Jake approached her. "We're in LA. Our fans are crazy here. That photo of us has surely pumped up the paparazzi. You shouldn't be going out alone. I'll go with you."

"No, I'm going alone."

Confusion washed over his face. "Why?"

"Because I'm a big girl and can take care of myself."

"Why do I feel like you're shutting me out again?"

"I'm shutting you out because I want to go out?"

"No. You're not telling me where you're going."

She glared. "Jake, let's get one thing straight here. I'm a grown-ass woman. I come and go as I please without you knowing my every move. We're not in a relationship."

His nostrils flared as he crossed his arms over his chest. "Trust me, Elle, I know. You make sure I don't forget."

The truth hurt, but she wasn't letting it show. "Great. Then there's no problem here, right?"

"Right."

"Seriously, Jake, we're just fucking. Stop acting all clingy." Elliot strode toward the house, holding back the urge to cry. She didn't want to be so mean, but it was much easier than telling him she was meeting Dax.

"Can you at least take security with you?" Jake called out, but she ignored him, continuing to the house. The quicker she got rid of Dax, the quicker she would get her life back.

14

*S*eeing Eli smiling back at her during a FaceTime chat always put Elliot in a good mood. He'd grown so much in the last four months. His blond hair was darker and closer to Elliot's natural dirty-blonde color. For a five-year-old, he was wise beyond his years and read her like a book. He'd sensed something was off during their call, even though Elliot had tried to hide it. She hated lying to Eli, but she wasn't ready to allow Dax back into their lives.

Some would chastise her for keeping Eli away from his father, but honestly, she didn't care. All that mattered was protecting her son from heartache. He was young and innocent, and she wasn't about to allow Dax to take that away from him. It would only be a matter of time before Dax would disappoint them both. That's what happened when your first love was drugs. The deal had always been that if he stayed clean, he could see Eli. And she knew how well that had gone.

But right now, her son looked happy and healthy with Sarah and her mom.

"Hey, peanut." Elliot held back the tears. "I'll be home real soon."

"I can't wait." Eli kissed his little palm with a smack of the lips, then threw her a kiss. "I love you, mama."

Elliot blew a kiss back. "Love you more, peanut."

The screen turned black as their call ended.

A knock on her bedroom door startled her. "Miss Phoenix, your car is ready." A man with a deep, raspy voice spoke from the other side. "Name's Mac." He slid his card under the door. "I'll be escorting you to your destination."

Elliot bent down and picked up his card. She rolled her eyes. *Mac Brown, Head of Security.*

"Mr. Quin sent me."

Of course, he had.

She opened the door to a massive mountain of a man wearing a black suit. His crewcut and goatee were peppered in gray. "I'm sorry, Mac, but I won't be needing your services tonight."

"Change of plans, Miss Phoenix?" Mac crossed his arms over his hulking chest. He stood in a wide stance, ready for any BS she threw his way.

"No changes. I just won't—"

"Excellent. I'll be waiting right here until you're ready." He puffed out his chest, letting Elliot know she wasn't going anywhere without him.

Jake! She shook her head as she exited and closed the door.

An hour later, Mac pulled into the driveway to Dax's penthouse in West Hollywood off Sunset Boulevard. Elliot sat in the backseat of the black Range Rover, debating whether to go inside like a big girl and take care of business or tuck tail and demand Mac drive away.

"Mac, stop here," she told the driver before they entered the parking garage.

Elliot looked out the window to the fifth floor. Dax's balcony. The air in her lungs seized as she recalled the day she'd left this place—the last time she'd used drugs. That was when she'd made a promise to herself to get clean, leave Dax, and start a new life. Little had she known she was pregnant at the time.

There had been yelling, threats to ruin her career, holes punched in the walls, and objects thrown. Elliot had seen a side of Dax that scared her. Thank God her sister had been waiting outside in the car for her. That night she'd left with nothing and never looked back.

"Miss Phoenix, is everything okay?" Mac asked as he looked at her through the rearview mirror.

On the outside, she looked strong, but on the inside, her stomach was knotted. She was on his turf, and they'd be alone. She took in a deep breath, returning eye contact with Mac. "Facing your ex-husband is never okay."

Mac nodded as if he understood. "They don't call them exes for nothing."

"True," she agreed.

"That bad?" Mac asked.

"The worst and best day of my life. I just don't know if I want to be alone with him."

His face grew grim. "Miss Phoenix, it's not my place to give you advice. I'm hired to keep you safe. However, you can't keep running from your problems. Your ex seems like a problem we can fix."

"We?"

Before another word was spoken, Mac drove forward to the security guard inside the parking garage. He gave the guard Elliot's name and who she was here to see. Given the okay, Mac parked. He got out of the SUV and opened her car door.

"Miss Phoenix, shall we?" He held his hand out, helping her out of the vehicle. Elliot was speechless. "What floor is your ex on?"

"Fifth floor," she barely said.

He motioned for her to take the lead as he followed her to the elevator.

Elliot punched in the floor number, then waited for the elevator. "Mac, you can stay in the car. I can do this on my own."

"Yes, Miss Phoenix, you can do this. I'm here for back-up." The mountain of a man showed no emotion. He stood there in his *Men in Black* suit and Aviator sunglasses, looking straight ahead. There was no doubt Mac was ready for anything coming their way. She bet if she searched him right now, the man would be packing some serious heat, which calmed her nerves a little.

Elliot stared at the silver doors of the elevator. On the drive over, she'd gone through multiple scenarios on how the conversation would go down. Dax was unpredictable, and she was the one who had everything thing to lose.

With a ding, the doors slid open, and Elliot walked into the elevator with Mac close behind. Her stomach knotted tighter the closer they got to Dax's place. When the elevator opened on his floor, she paused. Panicking, her feet wouldn't move. What was the harm in ignoring Dax, just like she had for the past five years? Then, she quickly remembered he'd tried to see Eli without her consent. And that was not going to happen.

Mac placed his hand on the small of Elliot's back, edging her forward. Without a word, she knew what Mac was doing. He was giving her the strength she needed to face Dax.

Elliot hadn't finished knocking on the door before Dax opened it. She was taken aback at how eager he was to see her. "Hey, you made it." Dax flashed her a wide take-your-breath-away smile. It quickly faded into a frown when he saw Mac standing behind her. "You brought a bodyguard?" His dark brows pinched together.

"Mac is a friend." Elliot pushed past Dax as she entered the penthouse. It hadn't changed much. Same cream-colored leather couches. The same musky smell of spilled beer soaked into the carpets. Same floor-to-ceiling windows that looked out on the West Hollywood skyline. She remembered many times when she was alone in the house. At night, she'd shut off all the lights and allow the glow of the skyline to light up the penthouse. She'd sit on those same leather couches and gaze into the electric horizon, making promises to herself that she was going to be the world's greatest female guitarist. Looking back now, she'd been so far away from reaching her dreams.

Elliot crossed her arms when she saw Dax give Mac dirty looks as Mac made himself at home, getting comfortable on the couch. "What do you want, Dax?"

Dax scratched his blond-bearded chin. "I can't get over the bodyguard, Elliot. Why did you feel the need to bring him? Are you scared of me?"

"This isn't about you. Why did you try to see Elijah?"

Dax walked over to the wet bar in the living room and poured himself a glass of whiskey. "Want one?" he smiled wickedly. He knew that offering her a drink would get under her skin, make her lose focus, and do something stupid. That's what Dax did to gain control of a situation.

Elliot held in a couple F-bombs. "I'm good." She tipped her chin up, keeping her composure.

Dax leaned against the bar and took a sip of his drink.

Elliot had to give it to him. He looked good. There had been a reason she'd fallen for him. He was tall, with muscles in all the right places. He was charming in his own heavy metal, lead-singer way. Yeah, she'd fallen hard for the long dirty-blond hair and rock and roll, bad-boy attitude. There had been a time she'd had fun tracing his tattoos with her tongue. And he had plenty to discover.

But she'd moved beyond that.

Stay on point.

"Elliot, you were ignoring me. You know I don't like to be ignored."

"How do you think I feel? You've ignored me and Eli for five years. So, no, I don't feel bad for you."

"Fair enough." Dax took another sip as he pinned her with his dark, sultry gaze. God, she hated that look. That look used to make her wild with desire. Now, she wanted to puke.

"You look good, Elliot."

"Stop wasting my time, Dax." She planted her hands on her hips. "What do you want?"

"Glad you asked." Dax set his glass down, then folded his arms. "I want to see my son."

Elliot's heart sunk. "You can't be serious."

"Sweetheart, I'm serious."

"I have full custody of Eli. You can't just show up and demand to see him. You left him. Hell, Dax, you were too wasted to make it to his birth. I should have left your name off the birth certificate. How do I know you won't leave him again?"

"That's not fair. You dropped the whole I'm pregnant bomb after you left me. I didn't know what to do."

"How about, instead of being a deadbeat dad, you support your family?"

"You know I didn't want a kid."

She glared, and if her eyes were lasers, they'd burn a hole straight through him.

"Listen, why can't we try again? For Eli."

"Why the change of heart?"

"Death Tribute broke up."

"I'm sorry to hear that." She really was. That band was his heart and soul. But was that his reason to want to see is child? He had free time now—time to spare? It wasn't going to work. Eli didn't need a part-time dad.

"It was a long time coming. Musical differences—"

"Drugs and alcohol abuse."

Dax rubbed the back of his neck. "Yeah, that's a fair assessment."

Elliot, still with her defenses up, watched him intently. She didn't trust him.

"You asked me what I want, and I want you and Eli in my life. I've changed, Elliot." He walked toward her, towering over her, making her feel small and vulnerable. "I have no more distractions in my life since the band broke up. I'm ready to settle down, be a dad." He rubbed her arms, and her body shivered in disgust. She averted her gaze to the floor as he stepped closer. "With you joining Gracefall, we'll be financially set."

And there it was. Dax needed money. How could he have pissed it all away? *The drugs.* Elliot squeezed her eyes shut. The nerve of him.

"Maybe I could even tour with you. You know, to take care of Eli. What do you think, sweetheart?"

Slowly, she opened her eyes and met his. She wrapped her arms tighter around her chest, concealing her fisted hands. "First, don't ever call me sweetheart. Second, you haven't changed. You're still the same egotistical asshole who only looks after himself. And third, my business with Gracefall is none of your concern."

Dax took a step back, probably shocked she'd spoken up. "Since when did you become a bitch, Elliot?"

Mac stood, obviously overhearing the conversation. Elliot nodded, telling Mac to stand down. Embarrassment began to flood her; good God, Mac was overhearing all of her drama. Could he be trusted not to share this with Jake?

Dax looked at Mac then back to her. "So, you think because you're clean now and have moved on to better things, you can cut me out?" He didn't give her time to respond. "You wouldn't have a career if it wasn't for me. I made you, sweetheart. Don't forget it." He walked back to the bar and grabbed his drink.

God, she was dancing on the edge of exploding. "You're an arrogant asshole. I worked hard to get where I am today."

"Yeah, you did." He winked with a wicked grin as he looked her over, clearly thinking dirty thoughts.

"That's it." Elliot threw her hands up. "I'm out of here. Let's go, Mac." She headed toward the door.

"Wait."

For some stupid reason, Elliot stopped before opening the door. She looked up at the ceiling, praying for patience. "You have five minutes."

"I was hoping we could be civil."

Elliot turned around. "What does that mean?"

Dax picked up a stack of papers on the dining room table and handed them to her. Elliot scanned the documents and paused briefly at the comment that described her as an unfit mother. She read on. He wanted full custody of Eli and a large amount of child support. "You've got to be kidding." Elliot slammed the documents on the table. "You have some nerve."

Dax leaned against the table and crossed his arms. "It doesn't have to be like this."

Elliot took in a deep breath before she lost her cool. "Look at me, Dax." He did. Dilated pupils, red eyes. Just as she suspected—cocaine. "Are you using?"

Dax looked away, which confirmed her suspicions.

"You're still using. Everything makes sense now." Elliot shook her head. "You need money to support your drug habit, and you're willing to use our son to get it from me."

Dax stood quietly.

Elliot picked up the documents. "Is this truly what you want?"

He said nothing.

"Fine, my attorney will be in touch." She headed toward the door, hiding the rage brewing inside her. This wasn't what she had expected. Deep down, she'd prayed Dax had gotten clean and truly wanted to be in Eli's life. She would have worked something out. Just because she and Dax weren't together didn't mean he couldn't see their son. However, he was using, and that was a huge problem.

"Go ahead. Have it your way. The tabloids love a juicy rock and roll drama. I'm sure I have some old photos of the good old days lying around. The press would love to get their hands on a wasted Elliot Phoenix."

Elliot froze before her hand touched the doorknob. Dread hung over her like a heavy dark cloud. Blackmail? Now this was a whole new level of Dax.

"I don't think you want those skeletons to come out. What would Eli think of his mother?"

She whipped around, pinning him with a hate-filled glare. "You have no idea what you are saying. Eli is off-limits to the media."

A sly smirk spread across Dax's lips. "You haven't told your new employer about Eli, have you?"

"It's none of your business, Dax. I will tell them when the time is right."

"Well," Dax huffed as if he were offended. "I think Joe and the guys deserve to know. Why haven't you mentioned him? Are you ashamed of Eli?"

Every fiber in her being urged her to march right up to him and punch him in the face. The man was toxic. She straightened her shoulders and lifted her chin. "You don't know mine and Eli's situation because you were never there. Everything I do is for Eli. Everything you do is to get the next fix. That, my dear, will not win you father of the year."

Dax raised his head, smoothing his hair from his face. Elliot noticed the hard lines creasing his face, the dark circles under his eyes, and his sunken cheeks. "He doesn't get to have you and Eli."

His low, deep voice sent a chill up her spine. "What are you talking about?"

"I saw the picture of the two of you online."

A lump formed in Elliot's throat. Was Dax playing the old jealous tactic? "You mean Jake?"

"Is that his name?"

His arrogance was really pissing her off. She'd changed since she'd been with Dax. The old her would have caved into his demands. No, he didn't get to manipulate her or Eli.

Elliot strode over to Dax, pinning him with a cold glare. "You don't get to tell me who I can fuck." She jabbed his chest with her pointer finger. "You don't get to tell me how to run my career. And don't ever question my ability to take care of Eli." She looked him up and down. "You're pathetic." Elliot whipped back around and headed toward the door. "Fuck off, Dax. I'll see you in court." She opened the door, wanting to slam it, but realized Mac was behind her. She heard Dax yell an obscenity or two to the tone of C U Next Tuesday.

Not wanting to wait for the elevator, Elliot sprinted down the stairs to the parking garage. She flung the door of at the bottom of the stairs open, almost ripping it off its hinges. She tossed the documents into the garbage can, then strode to the black Range Rover. The adrenaline rushing through her veins felt like liquid rage as she paced the length of the SUV. She fisted her hands, releasing some fury.

Fuck Dax Gage!

Elliot pulled out her phone and called Sarah, praying that she was home. Taking in deep breaths, she waited for her sister to pick up.

"Hey."

"Are you at work?"

"Just left. Elle, what's going on. You never call me after midnight unless it's an emergency."

Holding back the rage, Elliot exhaled.

"Talk to me."

"I just left Dax's house."

Her sister didn't say a word, but Elliot knew she was thinking the worse. " I didn't sleep with him and no, we're not back together."

Elliot heard Sarah exhale in relief.

"He's taking me to court for full custody of Eli."

"Are you kidding me?"

"It gets worse. He's not fighting for custody because he wants a relationship with his son. He's doing it for money."

"What do you mean?"

"He's broke, his band broke up, and he's still using. If he gains custody of Eli, I'll have to pay child support, which he'll use to fund his addiction."

"Asshole!" Sarah exclaimed. "I knew something was up when he showed up here wanting to see Eli."

"Sarah, Dax is to never be trusted with Eli. I don't care what he says."

"Absolutely."

"And don't tell mom. I don't want her worrying over this mess. I'll take of it."

"You know, Elle, you're not alone. We can help."

"I know and I appreciate it, but I'll handle it."

Elliot stopped pacing as she saw Mac walking toward her wiping his hands with a bloody white cloth. "I have to go. I'll call you soon."

"Okay. I love you and don't worry about Eli. I'll keep him safe.

Distracted, Elliot hung up without saying goodbye.

Confused, Elliot looked at Mac's hand. "Why is your hand bleeding?"

The mountain of a man opened the SUV's door for her. "No one in my presence disrespects a woman." He motioned for her to get in.

Still stunned, she got into the car. By the look of his hand, something had gone down.

Mac turned the ignition over as he looked at Elliot through the rearview mirror. "Sterling residence, I assume?"

Elliot nodded, flashing him a smile of thanks. Back to Melody's engagement party tomorrow; back to Jake. She was more thankful than ever that Jake had Mac chaperone her. Whatever had happened after she left Dax's, the bastard had it coming.

15

*O*ne o'clock in the morning and no sign of Elliot. Jake rolled over in bed, picked up his cell on the nightstand, and checked his text messages. Fuck. Mac hadn't returned his text, and neither had Elliot. Jake was trying to respect Elliot's privacy, but it was driving him crazy not knowing where she was. He thought that hiring Mac for the night to be Elliot's personal bodyguard and driver would mean he'd have an inside guy to report back to him. Wrong! He should have hired a private investigator. Seemed as though Mac respected Elliot's privacy.

Jake didn't want to come off like a creepy stalker; he wanted her safe. He'd seen how quickly a fan mob could form and how it could escalate into a frenzy when a band member is recognized in public. Alone, Elliot would be torn to pieces.

Jake knew Mac from the police force; he could be trusted. The big guy looked like a badass professional wrestler, but he was as gentle as a teddy bear. Jake had been surprised when Mac announced his early retirement so he could pursue private security. He would do whatever it took to get him on the Gracefall payroll.

When Elliot hadn't made it to dinner six hours ago, that's when the text messages had started. Mac texted back once, confirming Elliot was in the SUV with him. That was it. And why hadn't Elliot texted? Was she really that mad at him for wanting to know where she was?

After dinner, Jake joined the gang at the pool cabana where they'd hung out, enjoying a fire in the pit for a few hours. For the first time, Jake had felt a real connection with them, a friendship beyond being a temporary member of the band. The only thing missing was Elliot.

Melody and Joe were the first two to turn in for the night, which wasn't surprising. They could barely keep their hands off each other. It wasn't long after that Dylan had hauled Dani over his shoulder and headed inside. Jake would have been surprised if they'd made it to a bedroom. Then, only Cherry, Tyler, and himself remained. Everything had been cool, until Tyler had given Cherry bedroom eyes. Cherry stated her opinion with an "oh, fuck no" and went inside, leaving Tyler drunk and laughing his ass off. For some reason, he got a kick out of messing with her. Before Tyler gave Jake bedroom eyes, Jake retreated to his room.

Now, at one in the morning, he was alone and worried about Elliot.

Elliot wasn't his girlfriend. Yeah, he got that, but a simple "Hey, I'm fine" text would have been nice. "Shit." Jake scrubbed his hands down his face. He'd done something stupid. He'd fallen in love with Elliot.

Jake thought about her all the time, which hadn't been a problem when they were on the road. On the bus and on stage, they were always together. There were times he'd broken through her tough outer shell, and she'd let him see her softer side. That's what intrigued him. That's what he loved.

But there was something else going on with her. Jake felt it when she'd shut him out by the pool this afternoon. He couldn't help but wonder if Dax was the problem.

Jake blew out a heavy sigh as he rested his hands behind his head. Was Dax back in the picture? Was she still in love with him? Why should he care? She'd made it clear—no relationships. If Dax was back, Jake was out.

A knock on his bedroom door pulled him from his musing. "Hey, it's me."

He closed his eyes and exhaled, relived it was Elliot. Thank God she was all right. He cleared his throat, pulling himself together. "It's open."

Elliot opened the door and quietly shut it behind her. Her hair was pulled into a high ponytail, and she was wearing an oversized Gracefall concert T-shirt that left him wondering what she wore underneath.

Jake sat up, concerned. She looked nervous. "Elle, what's wrong?" He was ready to jump out of bed and go to her but stopped when she climbed in under the covers.

She laid her head on his chest and hugged him. "I'm sorry for what I said today by the pool."

Jake was stunned at her confession. It wasn't like her to apologize for things like that. He hesitantly kissed her forehead. "You're forgiven." He felt her exhale a shaky breath like she was relieved. "But I was worried about you when you didn't return my text."

Elliot hugged him tighter. "I was in a horrible place when you texted me. I know that's no excuse. I'm sorry that I worried you."

Jake wrapped his arms around her, comforting her from

whatever had her unnerved. Whatever it was, she could take it out on him.

Jake didn't push the question of where she had been, even though it was eating him up inside. They lay in silence as he waited for her to tell him on her terms.

He didn't know how long they had lain there before Elliot rolled over onto her back. By the moonlight shining through the window, he saw her staring up at the ceiling. Her chest rose and fell quickly as she licked her lips. "I went to see Dax tonight."

Jake's world was thrown off its axis. He had been right. He braced himself for the following line of "Hey, it's been fun, but I'm leaving you for Dax" because that's what always happened. He was the good guy women left for the bad boy.

"I wanted to tell you, but the last time the two of you met things got ugly."

"Yeah, good call."

Elliot grew quiet again. He didn't want to push her, but damn, he needed to know where he stood.

"Shit," Elliot exclaimed as she wiped her eyes with the back of her hands. "God, I hate him. Seeing Dax tonight brought back all the pain I've tried to overcome."

Jake lay there silent, listening to every word and tamping down the urge to visit Dax himself.

"He cheated on me countless times. I had believed it was my fault and took him back every single time. I was such a fool."

"Elle, you're not a fool. He's a manipulator. He took advantage of a kind-heart woman."

"No, Jake, I take full responsibility. I should have left him sooner than I did. If I had, I wouldn't have ended up an alcoholic and—" Elliot paused. Was she going to reveal something? "It doesn't matter. He broke me, and I allowed it."

Jake's heart ached for her. She needed to see she wasn't broken. Everything she'd gone through had made her stronger. He wished she saw what he did—a fun-loving, kick-ass guitar goddess who was so much stronger than she knew.

"Jake," Elliot's voice cracked.

"Yeah, baby."

"Dax is going to try to destroy me. He wanted to get back together, and I refused. All he wanted was my money to support his drug habit."

Jake rolled over onto his side, facing her. "He can't destroy you. I won't let it happen." He caressed her cheek. "Elle, look at me." The sorrow in her eyes about killed him. What he wouldn't do to take her pain away. "Dax is a junky."

She gave him a half-smile, which looked forced. "There's something else?" Jake pressed.

Elliot nodded. "Please don't ask me to talk about it. I will when the time is right."

"Fair enough." He leaned in, and their lips met. She plunged her hands into his hair, urging him to kiss her deeper. With Elliot, it didn't take much to turn him on. Her need was kindling the flames already burning inside him.

He pulled back to catch a breath. "Tell me what you want me to do."

She gazed deeply into his eyes. "Erase him from my brain."

He lifted her T-shirt over her head. She was beautifully naked, lying below him. "Show me where it hurts."

Elliot put her hands on his shoulders and gently pushed him down her body toward her sex.

Jake left a trail of fiery kisses as he made his way to where she wanted him. He spread her legs wide, then dipped his head between them. Christ, she tasted good. She awarded him with a moan.

"Is this where it hurts?" He licked her again, flicking his tongue over her clit.

"Fuck, Jake, right there," she begged.

Her plea drove him forward, harder and faster. Pleasing Elliot was the only thing on his mind. He was thoroughly enjoying erasing Dax from her brain.

Elliot's hips arched off the bed as she brought her legs around his head. Her body quivered. Fuck yeah, she was coming. Jake pushed her legs down, keeping her spread wide open for him as he continued sucking and licking until he ultimately brought her over the edge.

Knowing he made Elliot squirm with pleasure was all he needed. He didn't care if she didn't love him. To hell with it. She could take it all out on him. He was hers tonight to fuck away the pain. After tonight, Dax would be a distant memory.

$\sim$

*E*lliot wrapped her arms and legs around Jake as he held her. He nuzzled her neck. His touch was soft and gentle as she recovered from what she believed to be a once-in-a-lifetime, mind-blowing orgasm. Jake had left her breathless and floating in a fog of paradise.

The desire rekindled when Jake began kissing her neck and kneading her breasts. "You're the most beautiful woman I've ever met, Elle."

His words made Elliot awkwardly fidget inside. She'd never learned how to take a compliment gracefully. "You're not so bad yourself." She cringed at her lame execution of her feelings."

Jake shifted his attention to her breasts. "Not bad?" he said between kisses.

"You know what I mean."

"Do I? Tell me."

Elliot wasn't on the up and up on talking dirty in the bedroom. She was a more show don't tell kinda girl. But for Jake, she'd try her best. "Jake Quin, the master of my pussy." Okay, so maybe it wasn't her best effort.

Jake snapped his head up from her breasts and smiled wickedly. "I like that."

She returned his smile as she slid her hand between them and gripped his cock, slowly stroking him. "I should return the favor." She lifted her head and kissed his neck. Sex and the fresh scent of orange blossoms invaded her nose. The man smelled terrific.

He grabbed her hand and brought it to his lips. "Tonight is about you. I can wait." He kissed her hand.

Jake couldn't be more perfect than he was right now. He didn't take what he wanted. Instead, he cared about her, which was totally an oddity in itself. The contrast between Dax and Jake was like night and day.

"I know our little arrangement about fucking doesn't include feelings, but Elle, I care about you a lot. When you didn't call, I was worried something bad had happened to you. It drove me crazy not knowing."

She turned her head to the side, avoiding his smoldering gaze. Why did he have to go and ruin the moment?

"Elliot. Look at me." Jake placed his hand under her cheek and tilted her head toward him so their gazes met.

Shit!

Elliot took in a deep breath. Looking into Jake's eyes, she saw the truth. She saw a future she dared to dream of. But most of all, she saw the love in his blue depths. "I care about you, too." She caressed his bearded cheek.

Jake didn't say a word. A huge smile spread across his lips.

"What?" Elliot said shyly. "No one has ever said that to you before?"

"Only the one woman who matters the most."

She rolled her eyes. "You're so cheesy, but I like it."

"I think this is a good start, don't you?"

"I do." She bit her bottom lip to stop the silly grin from appearing on her face. But inside, she was as excited as a kid on Christmas morning.

Jake bent down and kissed her tenderly. "So, tonight is all about you. What do you want to do?"

"This." Elliot rolled him over, straddling him. She leaned down, her breasts pressed against his chest. She claimed his mouth, parting his lips with her tongue as she rocked her hips forward, sliding her sex back and forth along the length of his cock. God, he felt so good.

Jake grabbed her hips, holding her still. "Hold that thought." He reached over and grabbed a condom off of the nightstand.

She cocked a brow at Jake as he tore open the wrapper. "Were you expecting this?" She pointed at herself, then to him.

"No, baby, I always come prepared." He flashed her a wicked smile as he rolled the condom on.

"Well, preparation pays off." Elliot lowered herself onto his cock gently, taking every delicious inch of him in. Ecstasy filled her as he stretched her walls and made room for him. Elliot sat up, slowly rocking her sex up and down his long length.

"Fuck, Elle," Jake hissed.

The rhythm intensified, but Elliot kept the pace steady, slow, and easy. No way was she rushing this. Jake felt too damn good.

Sex with Jake lured her into another universe where, at the moment, nothing mattered. She didn't have to think, only feel. Nothing was complicated. They fit perfectly together like they were made for each other.

Jake moved his hand between them, rubbing her clit. She leaned back just enough not to break the connection, and holy fuck, he played her masterfully. Each stroke of his fingers pushed her further toward the edge. Elliot tossed her head back as she rode him nice and slow. "Jake," she moaned. "I'm going to come."

Jake growled like a feral animal, then pushed deeper inside her, tapping into another blissful sensation. One, two, three thrusts, and her body was no longer hers to control. She fell on top of Jake, still riding out the waves of her orgasm.

Having one orgasm during sex was greatly appreciated but two? Was there such a thing? With Dax, she was lucky if she had one at all. Jake made sure she was more than satisfied. God, she loved overachievers.

Jake pulled her in, wrapping his arms around her as she rode out the last wave. His body tensed. "Fuck," he sighed into her shoulder as he came. His timing had been perfect.

After freefalling out of that blissful universe, Elliot couldn't move, nor did she want to. She felt weightless, utterly sated, withered into a state of euphoria. Jake trailed feather-like caresses down her back and ass, keeping her body ablaze.

"That was fucking amazing." He kissed her shoulder.

She rolled over, and Jake discarded the condom. Elliot

brushed her sweaty hair from her face. "I've never come twice in one night before."

"Never?" His brows were raised as if in shock.

She nodded.

"Well, that's lazy." Jake lay down, pulling the sheets over them. He rested his arms behind his head. "Give me five, and we can break that streak." He turned his head and looked at her. "All in and double it." He winked.

Elliot scooted closer and laid her head on his chest. Strong arms held her, making her feel truly loved, relaxed... dare she say safe? "For the record, that would be four orgasms in one night."

"With you, baby, it's doable every time."

And she didn't doubt it.

"Elle." She felt his arms tighten and heard his heartbeat quicken.

"Yeah?"

"Stay with me tonight."

The sincerity in his voice went straight to her heart. Elliot looked up and met his sexy blue gaze, which rendered her speechless. She caressed his cheek and nodded.

He smiled, and his body relaxed. Jake kissed her forehead. No words needed to be spoken. It was there in his eyes; Jake loved her.

16

*J*ake walked into the engagement party with Elliot by his side feeling like the luckiest man alive. He was on cloud nine after last night's breakthrough with her, giving her four orgasms and waking up with her in his arms. Everything felt right in the world.

Elliot excused herself to find Melody as Jake claimed a spot at the open bar. He ordered a drink, then took in the lovely night. The air was cool and filled with savory aromas coming from the buffet. In the backyard of the Sterling mansion, people were gathered by the pool while waitstaff handed out flutes filled with champagne. Behind the pool, round tables covered in white linens and bright tropical floral arrangements dotted the area. There had to be room for at least a hundred people. A long buffet table filled with all kinds of food extended the length of the lush green hedge that framed the backyard. A canopy of white lights stretched above the pool to the tables, giving the appearance they were standing under the stars.

It was perfect.

The pool cabana had been magically turned into a stage,

where later Gracefall would play a song that Joe had written for Melody. Tonight would be the first time they would play it.

Again, it was perfect.

Jake's attention went straight to the happy couple, who were dancing in front of the pool cabana. The smiles on Melody and Joe's faces were intoxicating. They were crazy in love, and Jake couldn't be happier for them. One day that would be him and Elliot.

Perfect.

With love on the brain, he watched Elliot talking to Kimmy, her date, Davidson, and a redhead that Jake assumed was Ash, Dylan's ex-girlfriend. Elle looked beautiful tonight. Her blonde hair was down and hung straight, touching the tops of her breasts. He took in her off-the-shoulder black dress that accentuated her curves. Jake continued his perusal down to her long, tanned legs and her black stilettos.

Fucking perfect.

Elliot caught him staring and smiled. She mouthed, "Oh, my God. Four orgasms." She held up four fingers.

Jake snickered. If it were up to him, he'd do it again tonight. He nodded his head toward the bar, motioning for Elliot to join him. She excused herself and made her way to him. As he watched the sway of her hips and the way she glowed tonight, indeed, everything in the world was perfect. At least for one night.

"Hey." She kissed his cheek. "Thanks for rescuing me."

"My pleasure." He snaked his arm around her and pulled her close, stealing a kiss. "Have I told you how beautiful you are tonight?"

Jake loved the way her cheeks blushed. "Yes, but you can tell me again."

"You are stunning." He nuzzled her neck.

"You're pretty handsome yourself." She played with the lapels of his dinner jacket.

"So, how's Melody holding up?" Jake asked.

Elliot exhaled. "She's good. She was worried about her mother being here tonight, but it looks like the God of Thunder is on his best behavior." She tipped her chin toward Melody's parents, who were standing together, talking peacefully.

"Hopefully, they stay cordial. For Melody's sake."

"Being cordial toward your ex-husband isn't an easy task. I feel bad for Melody's mom. But they look like they're on their best behavior for their daughter."

Quickly, Jake thought of a way to change the subject. He'd didn't want to give Dax a chance to slip into Elliot's thoughts. Not tonight. "So, I think we should have a repeat of last night."

Elliot wrapped her arms around his neck. "I'll meet you in your room after the party?"

"The door will be open." He winked, then leaned in, claiming another kiss.

"For fuck's sake," Tyler exclaimed, interrupting.

Elliot hid her laughter behind Jake's shoulder.

"Hey, Tyler." Jake couldn't wipe the grin from his face.

Tyler ordered a drink, then looked them up and down. "You two are fucking."

Neither Jake nor Elliot denied it.

In his cool Tyler way, he tossed his long, curly chestnut hair back and leaned his hip against the bar, resting his arm on the table. "I don't care, as long as it doesn't bring drama into the band for the next two months."

"It won't," Elliot assured.

Tyler eyed them both again. "You know only one of you will make the cut, right?"

"We do." Jake looked at Elliot, and she nodded.

"Hell, do what you want. As long as it's not me in a relationship." Tyler threw back his double shot of whiskey. "I'm going to need another before going on stage and playing a sappy love song. I mean, I'll do it for Joe and Melody, but you two," he pointed to them, "don't fucking ask. The answer is no."

"Tyler, it's not like that," Jake assured.

"Yeah, we're not in a relationship," Elliot added.

"So, you're just fucking?" Tyler shook his head. "Shit, not my business."

Jake and Elliot shared a knowing look before Jake began to answer.

"Oh, look at the time." Tyler looked at his watch. "We've got to head over to the stage."

Jake did a quick time check. "Yep."

They headed toward the stage, where Joe and Dylan were waiting for them.

Dylan was chewing on his thumbnail, pacing back and forth. Jake prayed that he wasn't high, but Dylan was drunk and coked out by the look of things.

"Are you ready to do this?" Joe asked, acting nervous.

"Yeah, we got you, bro." Tyler clenched Joe's shoulder before walking on stage. Joe followed, then Elliot. Jake stood back, waiting for Dylan.

"Bro, you all right?" Jake asked Dylan.

Dylan cracked his neck from side to side and shook his arms, loosening up. "Yeah, never better."

Coked out and drunk, Dylan was dangerous. To add to the fire, he looked irritated. There was nothing Jake could do to help. He didn't have time to sober Dylan up.

Dylan shoved his finger at Jake's chest. "Listen, don't look at me like that."

Jake threw his arms in the air. "I'm not."

Dylan pointed at Jake, shooting him a glare before walking onstage. "Fuck you, Jake Quin."

Onstage, everyone took their places; however, Jake kept his eye on Dylan. He looked out into the audience as he positioned and tuned his guitar. In the front row, Melody stood with Dani, and she had a huge smile on her face as she looked at Joe behind his drumkit. Jake's stomach flopped as the rock legend, Leo Sterling, stared back at him from the audience. Leo had influenced lots of musicians over the last thirty years of his career. It was an honor for Jake to play for Leo's daughter and the God of Thunder himself.

Jake followed Joe and Tyler's cue and began playing the rhythm. He glanced to his right, and Elliot gave him a reassuring smile as she positioned her guitar strap across her shoulder. Everything felt good until Dylan, still looking like something was amiss, walked up to the mic stand. He cupped his hands around the mic and closed his eyes as if he were trying to push aside whatever was bothering him and sing the song.

Dylan shook his head. He stepped back and motioned behind him for Joe to stop playing. "Sorry, bro, this isn't happening."

The tension in the air was so thick Jake could barely breathe. This wasn't going to end well.

Jake spun his guitar so it rested on his back. He grabbed Dylan's shoulder. "Hey, don't do this. It's Melody's night."

Dylan shoved Jake. "Don't tell me what to do." Dylan pushed his hands through his long-haired mohawk as he paced the small area in front of the drums. "Fuck," he exclaimed, seemingly frustrated with himself. Dylan strode to the mic, and as he did, he took in a couple deep breaths. He looked at Melody, who looked confused and devastated. "Mellie, I'm sorry."

Jake looked over at Joe, who looked as if he was ready to pounce on his brother at any minute.

Dylan glanced at the floor as he stood behind the mic stand. He scratched his bearded chin. "Folks, I'm supposed to sing a song about love and how love conquers all." He shook his head and glared out over the guests. "I can't. I can't fucking do it. I can't sing about something I don't believe in." He glared at Ash, his ex, who was standing next to Davidson. "She'll tell you that she loves you, then she'll rip your heart straight out of your chest when you're not looking. When things get old, she places all the blame on you when you know damn well it takes two to rumble. Isn't that right, Ash?"

Jake watched the redhead shove her way through the crowd to leave.

"That's right, Ash, leave. That's what you're good at. You'll always be a ho!" Dylan yelled.

"That's enough." Jake grabbed Dylan's shoulder. "Joe is going to kill you."

Dylan turned to Joe. "Run, Joseph. They're all hos."

Joe charged Dylan, slugging his brother straight in the face. Jake caught Dylan as he stumbled back. "Get him out of my sight," Joe snarled, inches away from little bro's face.

The drummer stormed off the stage and up to Melody. With tears in her eyes, Melody turned away from Joe and strode inside.

Fuck. How could a perfect night turn into a such a shit show?

If he were being honest, Jake knew how...Dylan Grace.

◜

*J*ake held Dylan up as they parted through the sea of dirty looks the guests were shooting them. They'd made it to Dylan's room without another confrontation.

Jake sat Dylan on the edge of the bed. Dylan's head slumped over, and he lethargically laughed. "Did you see the look on her face?"

"Which one? You pissed off a lot of people tonight, bro." Jake poured a glass of water from the faucet in the bathroom and returned. He handed the glass to Dylan. "Drink."

Dylan pushed the glass away. "I was talking about Ash."

"I did, and I also saw the look on Melody's face." Jake stood in front of Dylan, observing his condition. "What are you on?"

Dylan swayed, then fell forward, passing out.

Jake caught him. "Hey." He shook him. "Dylan, wake up."

Dylan opened his eyes and mumbled something Jake couldn't understand. "Bro, don't fall asleep. We need to sober you up."

Dylan flopped back into the bed, laughing. "You can't save me, Jakey."

Jake had to do something. He had no idea what Dylan had taken or how much. Whatever it was, it was a lot. "Listen." Jake sat Dylan up. "I'm going to grab you some coffee. Promise me you'll stay put and not fall asleep until I get back."

Dylan was trying hard to look at Jake. His eyes were squinted, and his head swayed. "Jakey." He laughed. "Jakey...nakey—"

"Nope. That's not sticking, bro." Jake walked toward the door. "Sit. Stay. I'll be right back."

As Jake shut the door, he heard Dylan barking like a dog. It would be funny if Jake didn't have a bad feeling about the lead singer's condition. He had never seen him this loaded before.

Jake jogged down the stairs. As he reached the foyer, Elliot was there. "Hey, I was just going to check on you. How's Dylan?"

"Not good." Elliot fell into step with Jake as they made their way into the kitchen. "He's loaded."

"Shit."

"Yeah, I need to sober him up."

"Coffee?"

"Yep."

"Here, let me help." Elliot found the state-of-the-art coffee machine on the center island. She grabbed a K-cup and placed it in the coffee maker as Jake paced the kitchen.

"This is crazy." Jake buried his hands in his hair.

"Welcome to rock and roll, Pretty Boy." Elliot shot him a lopsided grin. "Okay." She waited for the last drop before taking the coffee mug from the machine. "We're done." She handed the cup to Jake.

He leaned in and kissed her cheek. "Thanks, babe."

Jake turned on his heels, leaving the kitchen, and Elliot followed. "I'm going with you."

"I'm not sure you'll want to see Dylan in his current condition."

Elliot gave him a knowing glare. "Are you serious? You know who my ex-husband is."

"Fine, but don't say I didn't warn you."

Jake opened Dylan's bedroom door and froze. Lying on the bed, Dylan was passed out cold.

"Fuck," Jake dropped the coffee cup, the hot, black brew splattered on the floor. He rushed to Dylan, praying that he wasn't too late. Jake sat him up. "Dylan." He shook Dylan. "Wake up, bro. Come on."

Nothing.

"Fuck!" Jake continued to shake, slap, do whatever he could think of to wake Dylan up.

"Does he have a pulse?" Elliot asked. Jake had asked himself the same question as the situation turned from bad to worse.

He paused and checked Dylan's wrist, then his neck. "I can't find one."

He laid Dylan down and pulled out his phone. "I'm calling 911."

"Wait." Elliot checked Dylan's pulse. And what seemed like hours later, she announced, "It's faint." She opened his eyelids. "His pupils are small." She laid her head on Dylan's chest. "Slow heartbeats." She reached into her purse and pulled out a bottle of NARCAN nasal spray. "Opioid overdose." She administered the spray up Dylan's nose.

Jake hung up the phone and stared at Dylan. A memory flashed before him. He was sitting on the ground outside of an apartment building holding his father's lifeless body. Tears streamed down his face as he apologized for not showing up sooner. There was nothing he could do or say to bring his father back.

A wave of helplessness hit Jake as he waited for Dylan to respond.

Dylan couldn't die.

Elliot resprayed Dylan. "Being a retired cop, you know CPR, right?"

Jake nodded.

"If this doesn't work, he may need CPR."

Like life being breathed back into the dead, Dylan's eyes shot wide open as he gasped in a rush of air. He sat up, coughing. "I don't feel good."

Elliot rushed to keep Dylan from slumping over. "You've overdosed. We need to get you to the hospital."

"I'm going to be sick." Dylan leaned over the side of the bed as Jake grabbed the nearest garbage can. He brought it over to Dylan just in time, saving the carpet from vomit.

Dylan sat up, resting against the headboard. He wiped his mouth with the back of his hand. "I'm not going."

"You have to go," Elliot insisted. "What and how much did you take?"

Dylan shrugged, which pissed Jake off. "If you don't tell me right now, I'm going to rip this place apart until I find it."

"Fuck," Dylan shoved his hands through his hair. "I did some coke."

Jake shot Dylan a "hell no, I'm not buying that story" look.

"Okay." Dylan let out a frustrated breath. "A lot of coke."

"And what else?" Jake pushed.

"Shit, dude, you're going all cop on me." Dylan raised his hands in front of him. "Cuff me. It wouldn't be the first time."

Jake leaped onto the bed and pinned Dylan down.

"What the fuck, dude!" Dylan squirmed underneath him, but Jake had the upper hand.

"Listen here, you little shit," Jake snarled. "You fucked up. Big time. You scared the shit out of Elliot and me. I thought you were dead. Elliot saved your ass. The way I see it, you owe her. You're going to the hospital. Or I can call Joe and have him deal with you. Your choice."

"Fine. I'll go. Just get off me."

Jake sat next to Dylan, both resting against the headboard, their breathing labored. Jake turned his head toward Dylan. "Don't ever do this to me again." He caught his breath. "I watched my father die, and I won't stay around and watch you die, too."

"I'm sorry." Dylan stared into his lap like a boy who had been scolded.

"Hey." Jake bumped Dylan's shoulder with his. "I'm here for you."

"Me too." Elliot sat on the edge of the bed next to Jake.

"Elliot," Dylan said, sounding tired. "Thank you for saving my ass."

Elliot nodded.

"How did you know what to do, Elle?" Jake asked as he came down from all the adrenaline pumping through his veins.

"Remember, I was a member of Death Tribute and married to a drug addict." Elliot flashed the bottle of NARCAN. "Never leave home without it. Plus, my sister is a nurse."

"Good thing. How many times have you had to use it?" Jake was seriously impressed by Elliot's calm demeanor throughout the situation.

Elliot shrugged. "Let's just say it was my job security."

They laughed.

"Seriously, though, I'm calling for an ambulance. We should let the rest of the band know what's going on." Elliot stood and slid open her cell. "I'll make the calls. Jake, you stay here with Dylan. Keep Joe from killing him."

"I guess I have no say in this at all," Dylan said.

Both Jake and Elliot replied. "No."

17

*J*ake and Elliot sat in the waiting room with Dani and Tyler while waiting for the doctor to clear Dylan for visitors. Jake wasn't leaving until he saw him.

"You know he's not going to agree to Davidson's terms." Tyler sat on the edge of his seat, resting his arms on his thighs. "He won't go to rehab."

"He will if he wants to continue being Gracefall's lead singer," Joe announced as he walked into the waiting room with Melody. They both looked emotionally drained. Melody had puffy eyes like she'd been crying.

Dani shot out of her chair and hugged Melody. "Are you okay? Stupid question. Of course, you're not."

"I'll be fine. How's Dylan?" Everyone looked at Melody in surprise. "What? Yeah, he ruined my engagement party, but I don't wish him harm."

Joe worked his jaw, not saying a word. Jake couldn't quite tell if big bro was pissed or worried about his brother. Perhaps a little of both.

"Dylan had his stomach pumped over an hour ago," Jake

said. "Doc said he'd be fine, but they wanted to follow up with a psychiatric evaluation."

"Are you sure they said psychiatric evaluation and not a priest?" Joe exhaled as he sat down next to Tyler. "With the demons that boy carries around, he'll need an exorcism."

Tyler snickered. "I'm glad you decided to come, bro."

"I wasn't going to. Melody talked me into it."

"Joseph Grace?" A brunette in a white lab coat asked.

Joe nodded and gave her a nonchalant wave.

"Hi, I'm Dr. Williams," she introduced herself. "Your brother is fortunate. I'd like to keep him overnight for observation while the toxicology report comes in."

"Not a problem," Joe answered.

"He can have visitors now."

Joe looked up and around the room as if saying, "Not me."

"I'll go." Jake stood.

"Me too." Elliot followed.

"Me too," Dani said as she paused from pacing. Jake felt bad for her; she hadn't sat still since she'd arrived. "I need to see him."

Tyler walked over to Dani and put his arm around her. "He'll be fine."

They followed the doctor down a long hallway with white marble floors and white walls. Dr. Williams stopped outside of a light-blue curtain pulled across the doorframe. She looked at her watch. "I can give you an hour."

"Thank you." Jake shook the good doctor's hand.

Jake pulled back the curtain, and Dylan was lying in the hospital bed with an IV attached to his arm.

"Hey, Jakey," Dylan announced, sounding a bit too chipper.

"No." Jake pointed at Gracefall's front man dressed in a

blue and white striped hospital gown, which was tucked in from the waist down. "I told you no Jakey." He looked Dylan over. "You look like shit."

Elliot pushed past Jake, giving him the side-eye. "Well, at least he's alive." Elliot bent down and hugged Dylan.

"Yeah, maybe on the outside, but after that mind fucking from the hospital psychologist, I feel pretty dead inside."

Dani walked in, and Dylan held his hand out to her. "You came."

"Of course." She took his hand and smiled at him sweetly. "Hi."

"Hey." Dylan smiled back.

"We need to talk." Tyler stood at the end of the hospital bed with his tattooed arms crossed over his chest.

Dylan looked at the door as if he were expecting more visitors. He rested his head back and closed his eyes. "Do we need to do this right now?"

"Yes," all four shouted.

Dylan shot a glare at Tyler. "So, since Joe isn't here, I guess he sent you in to his dirty work. I'm out of the band, aren't I?"

"That depends," Tyler stood firm. "You going to rehab?"

All the air in Jake's lungs seized. The future of Gracefall and possibly his career with the band laid in the hands of Wildman Dylan Grace. This wasn't good. Jake glanced at Elliot standing next to him. She kept her eyes on Dylan as she reached for Jake's hand. She squeezed it, letting him know she felt the same way. He had to convince Dylan to go to rehab. Not only for the band but for his own wellbeing.

"I think—"

"No!" Dylan cut Jake off. He shook his head. "I'm not going to rehab." He turned to Dani. "Please tell them I'm not going."

"Dylan, it's for the best," Elliot added. "We're all here for you."

"Fuck no. You all have no idea what's best for me. Besides, I can't leave the tour to go to rehab. I'm not going."

"Listen." Tyler sat on the edge of the bed. "This is coming down from the record label. Rick has noticed a decline in record sales and a change in your attitude."

"My attitude? Oh, that's rich."

Jake whipped out his phone. "Someone leaked a photo of you in the back of the ambulance. It's all over social media. Here's what your fans are saying from your fan page." Jake glanced up at Dylan before he started. "And I quote…

"Dylan Grace, a disgrace.

"What a waste. Gone too soon.

"Overrated. Typical rock star junkie. A waste of talent.

"Lame!"

Jake looked up from his phone. "Shall I go on?"

"Fuck social media. They can fuckin' suck it. They don't know me."

"Then prove them all wrong," Jake pressed. "Get clean."

Dylan avoided Jake and gazed out the window.

Elliot handed Dylan a royal-blue medallion. "This is my five-year sobriety chip."

A shocked expression came over Dylan's face. "I had no idea you were an addict."

Elliot took Dylan's hand in hers. "You have to get clean. It's your responsibility to Gracefall, but most of all, you owe it to yourself. It's not easy. That's why I'm offering to be your sponsor. You can't do this alone."

Dylan's gaze fell to his lap. "Dani, please don't make them take me away."

"You have an amazing opportunity here." Dani sat

beside Dylan and put her head on his shoulder. "I thought I had lost you."

Dylan laid his head back and exhaled. "Fuck Dani, no need to get all emotional. Hell, I'll go." He kissed her forehead.

A grunt came from the door. All eyes were on Joe as he stood in the doorway. He nodded at Dylan then walked away. How long had Joe been there listening? Jake didn't know, but he was glad Joe had come, and by the look on Dylan's face, he was, too.

18

*G*racefall, minus Dylan, sat in Davidson's office at Clef Tonic Records discussing the future of the band. Elliot wasn't surprised when it had been announced that the last leg of the tour was going to be on hold due to Dylan going into rehab. It was for the best for Dylan and Gracefall, but it also meant she'd have to wait longer to know if she got the job as Gracefall's lead guitarist. It also meant she'd get to spend more time at home with Eli.

Elliot's gaze landed on Jake, who was sitting across the table from her. His muscular arms rested on the table as he listened intently to Davidson. Her mouth went dry as she traced her eyes up to his bulging biceps, which strained against his black T-shirt. Just this morning, she was wrapped up tight in those wonderfully strong arms. No shot of whiskey or pill could replace the warm and fuzzy feeling she got when she was in Jake's arms. He was her new addiction.

Yeah, love had crossed her mind this morning. And this time, she didn't push the thought away. She was totally feeling it.

Sadness churned in Elliot's stomach as she thought about not seeing Jake. Without the band, nothing was keeping them together. How would she feel if Jake went home and fell in love with another woman? The thought made her heart ache. The reality was that he was free to date who he wanted, and she was free to date who she wanted. However, there was only one shaggy-haired, sexy rocker she wanted to bring home to meet the family. But was she willing to take that step?

Could she let Jake go?

Jake caught her staring at him and smiled. His electrifying blue eyes melted her insides and made her heart skip a beat. Fuck, she was in love. And it was different this time. With Dax, she was more in love with his lifestyle and the star than the person. Jake was what real love was all about—having someone who would stand by you no matter what. He'd already proven himself a solid person, lover, and man in so many ways.

The meeting adjourned, and Jake quickly made his way to the elevators. Elliot had to jog to catch up. "Hey."

He tipped up his chin.

"Looks like we're getting a vacation. Are you sticking around Cali?"

"No, going home," he said dryly.

Something was wrong. Why the cold shoulder all of the sudden? "Yeah, me too."

She waited for him to say something more or at least look her way, but he stared at the silver doors, rocking back on the heels of his boots.

The elevator ride to the parking garage was no better. Complete silence. It wasn't like Jake to ignore her. What had changed?

Why couldn't she open her mouth and talk to him? She

realized it was because this was when they parted ways. She didn't want to hear Jake say, "Hey, it's been cool," then watch him walk away. Perhaps it was better this way. At least she knew where she stood before she'd poured her heart out to him.

Elliot straightened her spine, walking a bit taller to the car waiting to take her back to the Sterling estate. She got into the backseat of the black SUV, leaned back, and exhaled. Love was for suckers. Thank God she hadn't fallen for the trap.

The long car ride back to the God of Thunder's estate gave Elliot time to ponder the situation, which added fuel to the fire. She wasn't angry at Jake. He'd followed her agreement. She was more furious at herself for putting him through her ridiculous no relationship rules, which she now regretted. But hey, that's what she'd wanted, right?

There was no going back. Tomorrow morning Elliot would be on a plane heading home to her son. Elliot didn't have time to think about what might have been with Jake; Dax Gage was breathing down her neck. She needed to hire a lawyer and clean up the mess her ex was dragging her through.

As soon as the car parked, Elliot hopped out and went inside. She headed up the flight of stairs that curved toward the second floor to the bedrooms. She strode down the hallway, and without thinking, she stopped outside of Jake's room. The right thing to do was talk to him, but she could not will her hand to knock on the door. She couldn't say goodbye.

Elliot cursed herself a coward as she continued down the hallway. She strode inside her room to the closet and pulled out her suitcase and duffle bag. In a hurry, she packed her clothes. There was no reason to rush. Her flight left in the morning. But just like that night when she'd left Dax, the overwhelming feeling of leaving swept her away. She couldn't stay here.

She grabbed her phone and called a cab. In her haste, Elliot realized she had no idea where she would go. Maybe she'd head to the airport and find a hotel nearby. Or just drive home. She paused to calculate how long it would take to get home when someone knocked on her door. "Hey, Elle, it's me, Jake."

Her gaze flew to the door as her frazzled brain froze.

"I know you're in there. We need to talk."

His low voice rattled her heart. She took in a deep breath and wiped her hands down her denim-covered thighs. She could do this; Jake was never hers to keep.

Elliot ran her fingers through her hair quickly and straightened her white tank top as she made her way to the door. She cracked the door open and peeked her head out. "Hey."

He looked at her strangely. "Umm, can I come in?"

She opened the door and let Jake in. "Make it quick. I have a cab on the way."

Jake did a quick sweep of the room. He glared at her suitcase and duffle bag by the door. "I see you're packed and ready to go."

"Yeah." Elliot shoved her hands in her front pockets. "I don't like to wait until the last minute to pack."

Jake nodded. "I hate packing. I throw all my shit in a bag as I'm heading out."

"Why are you here, Jake? I know you didn't pop in to talk about packing suitcases."

"Right." He rubbed the back of his neck. "I...ah, didn't mean to rush out of there." He hesitated as if trying to find the right words. "I've been trying to figure out what to say since we found out about the tour ending sooner than expected."

"Jake, there's nothing to say. No strings attached. We agreed. We can go home and never look back. Then, in a month, we'll know who Gracefall picked to be their lead guitarist. One of our dreams will come true, just like we planned in the beginning."

Fuck. What was she saying? This wasn't what she wanted at all. But there was no way he was getting to say goodbye first.

"So, you're telling me nothing has changed for you?" Jake's sorrowful blue gaze shot daggers to her heart.

Elliot stared back. "Has something changed for you?"

Jake exhaled. "Elliot, you know it has. You've known how I felt about you since day one."

Elliot's cell phone buzzed on the dresser. She picked it up. "My cab is here. I have to go."

"Fuck the cab." Jake grabbed her phone and tossed it on the bed. "You're not leaving here until I say what I have to say."

Elliot crossed her arms. A part of her was relieved that Jake was making her stay.

"This whole *just fucking* deal is silly. It was pointless to think I could let you go. The only thing that wasn't silly was falling in love with you." He framed her face with his strong hands and rested his forehead against hers. "I don't want this to end, Elle."

Elliot's breath hiccupped in her chest as she fought back the tears. "Me either." She wrapped her arms around his waist. "I don't want you to go."

He claimed her lips, gently working up to a fevered hunger. She took him in, comforted that Jake wanted her in his life.

She broke the kiss. "And here I thought you were here to say goodbye."

Jake's brows pinched together. "What?"

"After the band meeting, you didn't say a word to me." She shrugged. "I just thought—"

"Elle, that was the last thing on my mind. I was trying to figure out a way to make you stay with me."

"I so suck at this."

Jake snickered. "I should have said something after the meeting. I guess I kinda freaked."

Elliot grew quiet. Jake wasn't going anywhere, which meant now was the time to take it to the next step.

"Hey." Jake backed up, concerned. "Everything okay?"

Elliot shoved her hands in the front pockets of her jeans. "I need to tell you something, but before I do, you need to know I've kept this secret to protect someone very special to me."

"Okay." Jake gave her his full attention. "What is it?"

"I have a son, Elijah Gage."

"You and Dax had a child?" Jake pulled his hand through his hair. "Wow."

"Yeah, I didn't know I was pregnant when I left." Elliot's gaze fell to the floor. "I was wondering if you'd like to meet Eli sometime."

Silence. Jake stood in silence. Not the reaction for which she had hoped.

"I mean, it's okay if not. I just dropped a bomb. I understand if you need time to think about it."

"Are you kidding? I'd love to meet the little dude." A smile spread across his face. "I'm honored that you want me to meet your son. Do you have a picture of him?"

Elliot sniffed back the tears as she nodded. "Yeah." She grabbed her phone off the bed and flipped through her photos. "Here." She handed the cell to Jake. "He's five years old and loves dinosaurs."

She watched Jake's reaction as he took in the photo. "Look at that blond hair." He looked up from the cell. "Elijah looks just like you."

"That's a good thing." Elliot smiled. "So, you want to meet Eli? I mean, we are a package deal."

"Absolutely," Jake exclaimed.

Before Elliot knew what was happening, Jake pulled her into a tight hug. "I can't wait to meet the little dude." He hit her with a smoldering stare. "This is awesome. I can call you a MILF."

Elliot glared. "You did not just call me a Mother I'd Like to Fuck."

"How about Hot Mama?"

"How about no," Elliot protested.

"It was worth a try." Jake took Elliot in his arms and kissed her deeply. "Thank you for bringing me into your life."

"Well, don't go telling everyone. The band doesn't know. Like I said, I've kept Eli a secret for his protection."

"My lips are sealed."

Elliot grinned up at Jake. "Good." She kissed him as he dragged her backward toward the bed. Yeah, life was good... really good.

19

*J*ake pulled up to Elliot's lake house, his passenger a ginormous stuffed T-Rex. "Well, Rex, we're here, buddy."

He hopped out of the truck and walked to the passenger side. All this time, the love of his life had only lived thirty minutes away. He opened the door and unbuckled Rex from the car seat, hoping the giant dinosaur would be a hit with Elijah.

After a week of FaceTime with Elliot and Elijah, Jake was ready to finally meet the little dude and hold Elle in his arms. He'd missed her like crazy. Elliot had thought it best to introduce Jake first by FaceTime, then in person, and she was right. Jake's last phone call to Elliot was chatting with Elijah about dinos and which ones would win in a mega dinosaur battle. Already, he liked the kid.

Jake walked to the front door, holding Rex in front of him. "Okay, buddy, let's make this happen." He rang the doorbell.

Behind the T-Rex, Jake couldn't see who answered the door, but he knew it was Elliot by the laugh.

"Oh. My."

Jake peeked out from behind the stuffed animal. "I found him on the side of the road hitchhiking. Thought I'd give him a ride."

"Eli," Elliot called behind her. "Someone is here to see you."

The shaggy-haired blond boy ran to the door. "Jake!"

Jake set the T-Rex down in time to catch Eli's hug. "Hey, little dude. I brought you something." He showed his new friend to Eli.

"My favorite," Eli shouted and hugged the dino. "Mom." Eli turned to Elliot. "Can I show Aunt Sarah?"

Elliot rustled the boy's hair. "Absolutely," she beamed. "Just make sure you don't scare her."

"I won't."

Jake and Elliot watched Elijah take off down the hall.

"He's a great kid," Jake said as Elliot turned to face him.

"Yeah, he's pretty awesome." Elliot stepped closer and wrapped her arms around his neck, hugging him tightly. "I've missed you."

Her body pressed against his, and it was all he could do not to drag her off to the bedroom. Jake nuzzled her neck, breathing in her welcoming scent. It consumed him. A week without touching Elliot...never again.

He held her gaze, then claimed her mouth. Her sweet taste washed over him like a warm summer breeze, causing the urge to deepen the kiss. God, he felt like a king holding her in his arms.

Elliot broke the kiss. "Wow, you really did miss me." She licked her lips as she caught her breath.

"Fuck yeah, I did." Jake couldn't take his eyes off her.

"You should come in and meet the family." Elliot took Jake's hand and led him inside.

"Your whole family is here?" He didn't know if he was ready to meet the parents.

"Kinda. My mom and sister."

"Cool."

Elliot led him into the living room, where her mother, sister, and Elijah were hanging out. The room had a fresh and clean vibe, painted in neutral colors. A blue couch sat in front of a wall of windows that overlooked the lake. In one corner of the room, toys spilled out of a wicker basket.

"Jake, this is my mom, Janet, and my older sister, Sarah," Elliot said, making introductions.

Jake saw right away where the Phoenix sisters got their good looks. "It's a pleasure to meet you, Mrs. Phoenix."

Janet stood and shook her head. "Divorced. Call me Janet."

"Absolutely."

"Well, I can see why my daughter talks about you a lot." Janet winked. "You are handsome."

"Mom!" Elliot exclaimed.

Jake turned to Elliot. "So, you talk about me, huh?"

"Only good things." Sarah stood and shook Jake's hand. "Nice to meet you, Jake."

Jake nodded.

"Hope you're hungry." Janet patted Jake on the shoulder. "I made a pot full of spaghetti and meatballs."

"Sound amazing, Mrs.—Janet."

"Relax, Jake. Elliot likes you; we all like you." Janet headed toward the kitchen. "Sarah, help me in the kitchen."

Sarah excused herself, leaving Jake alone with Elliot and Elijah.

"I like her." Jake glanced at Elliot. "She's cool."

"Yeah, I wouldn't be able to do what I do without them." Elliot sat down on the couch, and Jake followed.

He put his arm around her and loved the way Elliot snuggled against him. Her warmth soothed Jake's body and soul. "Have you ever taken Elijah on the road?"

"No. I've kept Eli out of the limelight. He stays here at my sister's house."

"I assumed this was your place."

"No. I live with Sarah. She's helped me so much in getting my career back on track. Eventually, I hope to bring Eli on the road with me when the timing is right."

"So, the band has no clue that you have a son?"

"Right. I didn't want anything to jeopardize getting the Gracefall gig. If I get the job, Eli and I can be together on the road."

Jake now fully understood Elliot's determination. She was doing it for Elijah.

"I know this is none of my business, but what does Dax say about it?"

Elliot shrugged as she held Jake's hand. "Dax has never given a shit about Eli or me. He was never there, not even when I gave birth."

"Wow, that's pretty low."

"It gets worse."

"What do you mean?"

"Remember the night I went to see Dax?"

"Yeah."

"He told me that night he's taking me to court to get custody of Eli."

"What?"

"Yeah." Elliot exhaled. "He wanted to get back together, you know, for Eli's wellbeing." Her tone turned sarcastic. "When I refused, he threatened me with custody papers."

"Are you kidding me?"

"I wish I were, Jake. He's pulling this shit because one,

he saw us on social media, and two, Dax thinks I'll land the Gracefall gig, and I'll be his cash cow. The worst thing is he's claiming I'm an unfit mother."

"Elliot, no way. Everything you do is for Elijah. He can't prove it."

"Well, I think he can. I don't own or rent my own place. I'm on the road a lot, which doesn't make me look like a suitable mother."

"And Dax being a drug addict makes him father of the year?"

"Of course not."

"Then you have nothing to worry about."

"I know." Elliot lowered her voce as she watched her son playing on the floor with his new T-Rex. "I have a great attorney, but still, it's drama that I don't need. I know Dax, and he'll do anything to make my life miserable."

"Elliot, I promise you, Dax will never get custody of Eli."

"How can you be so sure?"

"I'm an ex-police officer. I have friends that can make Dax's life a living hell."

Elliot looked up at Jake. "What are you saying?"

"I'm saying you have nothing to worry about." Jake slipped his finger under Elliot's chin and tipped her face so she looked at him. "Trust me." He bent down and claimed her mouth. At this moment, Jake understood love. He'd do anything for Elliot.

~

*E*lliot stood at the kitchen sink, drying off the dishes her sister had washed. Her mind kept shifting back to Jake and how charming he'd been during dinner. Eli really liked him, and her mother and sister had welcomed him into the family. He was perfect. Too perfect.

"Hey, is everything all right?" Sarah asked, bringing Elliot's attention back to the plate she'd been drying.

"Yeah, why?" Elliot kept her thoughts of Jake to herself.

"Oh, I don't know. You've only been drying the same dish for the past twenty minutes."

Crap! Elliot put the plate down.

"Jake seems like a great guy." Sarah plunged her hands back into the soapy water, scrubbing a pot. "You really like him."

"Is it that obvious?"

Sarah nodded.

"Have you ever craved someone? Not just for sex. But for their touch, kiss, voice, or even just their presence?"

"I know the feeling." Sarah sighed. "I wish I could find a guy to crave. I'm like a magnet for jerks."

They shared a laugh.

"Yeah, well, be careful what you wish for. You could end up with a Dax."

"True." Sarah handed Elliot the pot to dry. "Speaking of Dax, does he know about Jake?"

"Yeah, and he's pissed about it."

Sarah's brows wrinkled. Elliot saw there was something else on her mind.

"Hey." Elliot placed her hand on Sarah's shoulder. "What's wrong?"

"I'm worried about you, little sis. I don't want you to end up with another Dax."

Elliot shook her head. "No way. Jake is nothing like Dax."

"I know. But you and Jake are going after the same dream. Only one of you is going to make it."

"I know."

"So, you've thought this through?"

Elliot paused. Had she? She'd lost focus and fell in love with the enemy. Was she fooling herself into believing that whatever happens with Gracefall wouldn't change anything between her and Jake? Elliot shook her head. "If Jake gets the job, I'd be happy for him, and I know he'd be happy for me."

Sarah gave Elliot a lopsided smile and pulled her into a hug. "Jake's a nice guy, and I'm ecstatic for you. Things will work out for both of you. I just know it."

Elliot hugged her sister and prayed that she was right.

"Besides, he's so freaking hot." Sarah fanned herself. "Does he have a brother?" she joked.

Elliot laughed. "He has an older brother and lots of cop friends."

"Hot cops?"

"Haven't met them, but I'm sure one or two would fit the bill."

The sisters laughed.

"All this talk about hot cops, I should go check on Jake. I'm sure Eli has shown him his dinosaur collection." Elliot gave Sarah a smile. "Everything will be all right."

Her sister returned the smile. "I know."

Elliot walked into the living room, where Jake and Eli were sitting on the couch. She stood out of sight as she watched her sexy rocker show Eli a couple chords on the guitar. Eli had been born with a guitar in his hands. She wouldn't have had it any other way. It even shocked her how well he played. A pure natural.

Jake and Eli looked up and noticed Elliot standing in the doorway.

"Mama!" Eli ran over to her. "Look what Jake taught

me." Excitedly, Eli strummed the chords; the sound he made was just like Jake's.

"Wow, buddy!" Elliot exclaimed. "Now, you sound like a rock star." She looked over at Jake and smiled.

Jake set his guitar aside and walked over to Eli, ruffling the boy's shaggy blond hair. "He's amazing, Elle."

"Yeah, he is."

"I mean, it's no wonder. It's in his genes."

Elliot chuckled. "Seriously, it comes naturally for him." She bent down to Eli. "Hey, I think Aunt Sarah needs your help in the kitchen."

"Okay." Eli handed his mother his guitar. "But only if I can play more when I'm done."

"Of course."

Eli scampered off.

Elliot melted into Jake as he held her against him. He nuzzled her neck, and butterflies stirred in her stomach.

"I don't want to let you go, Elle." Jake kissed her neck.

"I don't want you to go." Elliot threaded her fingers through Jake's silky hair.

Jake slid his hands up her shirt. His fingers trailed up her back, lighting her skin on fire. The ache between her legs craved Jake's touch. There was nothing she wanted more right now than him, but she didn't want to confuse Eli. And she definitely didn't want Eli to walk in on them.

"Jake," she said breathlessly to the point she didn't recognize her own voice. "I don't think this is a good idea." Her skin turned cold as Jake's hand left her body. He took a step back, as if confused. "I mean, I want to ask you to stay over, but I can't. I don't want to confuse Eli. I'm not ready to answer his questions tomorrow morning during breakfast."

"Whew, I thought I blew it with your family."

"God, no. They love you. This is all new for me. I want to take it slow for Eli's sake."

"I completely understand. I'll go as slow as you need."

Elliot closed the distance between them. She placed her hands on his chest, feeling his warmth. "What if I come to your place?"

"Yeah, go pack a bag."

Elliot laughed. "No. Not tonight. How about tomorrow?"

"I can't wait." He slipped his hand under her jaw and brought her into a kiss. A kiss that left behind a promise of pleasure and one hell of a sleepless night.

20

*A*ll day Jake had been cleaning his apartment, making sure it was spotless for Elliot. By no means, he wasn't a slob, but he lived comfortably. So, washing the dishes and vacuuming the floors were top priorities, along with clean bedsheets.

No matter how involved the cleaning got, Jake couldn't keep Elliot off of his mind. He hadn't wanted to leave her last night, but he understood why Elliot hadn't wanted him to stay, and he wanted to do what was right for Elijah. Dax was a fool for not being there for his son. Eli was an incredible little dude, and Jake was ready to build a father-figure relationship with him.

Even though he was ready to jump into an instant family setting, it was essential that they take it slow. He'd made a lot of progress with Elliot. She finally trusted him, and that was something he didn't want to jeopardize.

Jake loved Elliot beyond his rocker-girl crush. He'd loved her the first time he'd seen her on stage. What was a guy like him doing with a heavy metal goddess? Jake shook his head and smiled. Lucky bastard.

As Jake finished tucking in the freshly laundered bedsheets, his doorbell rang. Excitement raced through his body as he hurried to the door. He opened it, expecting to see Elliot. Instead, Dominic, dressed in his police uniform, was standing in front of him with a grim expression.

The first thought racing through his mind was that this wasn't good. Typically, Dom showed up ready for the bar. Jake's brows creased. "Hey man, what's going on?"

"I hate to do this to you, but I know it had to be me delivering the news." Dom handed Jake a manilla envelope. "You've been served."

"What?" Jake opened the envelope and read the first page of the document. "Stacy wants a divorce," he said, shocked.

"I thought you'd taken care of that before you left." Dom walked inside and surveyed the apartment. "Smells like Mr. Clean took a shit in here. Expecting company?"

Jake nodded as he continued reading. Since meeting Elliot, he'd completely forgotten he was still married to Stacy. He'd spent years waiting for her to come home, never really believing she was truly gone. And now, he was free from that poor decision. However, old wounds still stung. She'd broken his heart.

"Hey man, you okay?" Dominic asked as he stood over Jake's shoulder, reading the divorce papers. "At least she wants to cut ties. No strings attached."

Jake held the papers to his chest. "Mind your own business much?"

Dominic raised his hands. "Sorry. Just trying to help."

"Look, Dom, I appreciate you trying to help. I'm just a little shocked."

"Why? You've had five years to get over her. It's about time."

"I know." Jake set the papers down on an end table next to the couch. "I should have taken care of this a long time ago. I guess I didn't want to prove Brian right for warning me about Stacy."

"You were pussy whipped. There was no telling you differently." Dominic clasped Jake's shoulder. "I have to get back to work. Catch up later?"

"Yeah. I have someone I want you to meet." Jake tried to hide a smile but failed.

"Oh, for fuck's sake. Haven't you learned your lesson?"

"Why can't you be happy for me? Elliot's the real deal."

Dominic shook his head. "When?"

"She's coming tonight."

"Bring her to the bar. I'll be there when I get off."

"Cool."

"Does Brian know?"

"Not yet."

"This should be good."

Dominic left, and Jake picked up the divorce papers and took a seat at the kitchen table. He flipped through the pages, reading line by line. Stacy wanted nothing except for him out of her life, which meant she must have found another guy to screw over.

Jake exhaled and leaned back in his chair. He didn't know what to think. Relieved, yes, but it bothered him not knowing why Stacy had left in the first place. What hadn't he seen?

Jake pushed the chair back and walked into the kitchen to find a pen. He was signing the divorce paper stat. He'd had more than enough time to get over Stacy. The nightmare needed to end.

❧

*A*fter finding a spot in the parking garage, Elliot impatiently waited for the elevator to Jake's apartment. Since he'd left the night before, Jake had been on her mind. Sleeping alone without his arms wrapped around her had been torture. All night she'd tossed and turned, craving his touch. A hundred times, she'd cursed herself for telling him he couldn't stay.

But today, Jake was all hers, and she wasn't wasting one second.

The elevator doors opened, and Elliot walked inside, quickly closing the doors behind her. She fidgeted with the strap of her overnight bag as she watched the floor numbers go up, bringing her closer to Jake.

The elevator stopped, and Elliot bolted out. She did a quick glance at the apartment numbers, then headed down the hall. Her feet couldn't move fast enough.

Finally, she reached Jake's apartment. She knocked on the door and waited for what seemed like forever. The door opened, and Elliot couldn't contain herself. She jumped on Jake, throwing her hands around his neck and wrapping her legs around his waist. She couldn't wait for "hellos" and "how are you doings." Her mouth was on his in desperate hunger.

The door closed behind them, then she felt Jake's hands on her ass, squeezing. She shoved her hands in his shaggy brown hair, loving the smell of his fresh and clean shampoo. Her body felt as if it was going to explode if she didn't have Jake right here, right now.

"Whoa, I'm loving this enthusiasm, Elle," he told her between kisses.

She laughed as she tugged at his shirt, and they made their way into the bedroom; her lips never left Jake's. Jake was like a drug. His touch was the fix she needed to chase the high. And God, she never wanted to come down.

Her back hit the bed with Jake on top of her. She tugged off his shirt, breaking the kiss as he removed it. He gazed down at her, his muscular arms flanking her head. Disheveled hair hung around his face, giving him a sexy rocker look. Hunger burned within his vibrant blue eyes. "Hey." He flashed her a sexy smile that sent a lightning strike straight to her sex. *Holy shit!*

She couldn't stop touching him as she ran her hands down his chest. "Hey," she said breathlessly.

Jake bent down and kissed her neck. The sensation had her body moving seductively against his. He slid his hands up her shirt, leaving fiery trails over her ribs. Her nipples hardened. She'd never wanted Jake as much as she did right now.

He threw her top on the floor. His hands palmed her breasts, kneading them over her bra. His thumb brushed over her nipple, and she couldn't hold back anymore. She wanted him hard and fast.

Elliot rolled on top of Jake. She ripped her bra off and started on the button of her jeans. "Jake, fuck the foreplay. I need you now."

Without hesitation, Jake unbuttoned his fly. They shimmied out of their jeans and underwear in a hurry, and Elliot was on top of Jake again. She leaned over and kissed his neck as she reached down between them and took his cock in her hand. "I've thought about you all night." She stroked him.

"Mmm, I've thought about you, too. But this is much better."

Elliot smiled, loving the fact Jake had been thinking about her.

The ache between her legs was unbearable. She rubbed her sex along his cock, trying to relieve the throb, but it only made her want him more.

"Fuck, Elle. You're so fucking wet."

"That would be your fault, Pretty Boy." Elliot grabbed a condom from the back pocket of her jeans.

"I see you've come prepared."

"I always do." She winked and began sliding the condom onto Jake.

She straddled Jake, guiding him in until he was completely buried. The pleasure of his cock stretching and filling her fed her craving. "Jake," she moaned.

"Yeah, baby."

"I need you to fuck me."

Apparently, she didn't need to tell him twice. Jake held onto her hips and thrust deep inside her. He pumped her hard and fast, exactly the way she wanted it...needed it. She matched him thrust for thrust, chasing the ultimate high, which only Jake could deliver. She needed his touch, the closeness of their bodies. Something primal took over. She wanted everything Jake was giving and more.

Elliot was on the edge of ecstasy as Jake sped up the pace. He knew her body and knew she was ready. She quivered.

"That's it, Elle, come with me." Jake pumped her faster.

Her head fell back as Jake took her higher and higher. Jake's body stiffened at the same time her orgasm hit her hard.

She collapsed on top of Jake, out of breath. He held her tight and kissed her cheek. "That was fucking amazing."

Elliot agreed but couldn't find the words to say so without sounding like some lovesick fool. Fuck it, she *was* a lovesick fool. "I love you, Jake," she mumbled against his neck.

An uncomfortable silence filled the room as she waited for Jake to say it back. Elliot wasn't expecting him to say it, but she hoped he would. She rolled over onto her back and stared at the ceiling as Jake cleaned up. "I didn't mean to get all weird on you."

"Weird?" Jake lay down, turning his head toward her. She met his gaze.

"I'm sorry."

"Elle." He rolled over on his side and caressed her cheek. "I've loved you since the first day we met."

Elliot smiled as tears filled her eyes. She was so happy, like she was floating on cloud nine.

"I love you." Jake leaned in and kissed her gently. "And if you greet me like this every time you come over, you can ring my doorbell anytime." He flashed her a wicked, sexy smile that melted her insides.

She rolled over, facing him, and wrapped her arms around him. "I'll make a note of that."

"Tell me again."

Elliot knew what Jake wanted to hear, but she played it off. "Tell you what?" She grinned.

"Tell me you love me." His playful jokes turned sober.

"I love you, Jake Quin." His mouth came down on hers with so much passion that it left her breathless. So, this was love.

Elliot snuggled against Jake's chest as they both dozed off, fully sexually sated.

～

"*H*ey." Jake caressed Elliot's back. "Are you up?"

Elliot, still wrapped in Jake's arms, stirred. She couldn't believe she'd fallen asleep. Being in Jake's arms relaxed her. Nothing in the world mattered. She stretched. "Yeah, how long was I out?"

"Not long. An hour."

"That long? Why didn't you wake me?"

"You looked so peaceful. I didn't want to disturb you."

God, Jake was perfect. "Thank you." He kissed her. "Mind if I make some coffee? I need to wake up."

"Help yourself."

Elliot hadn't realized just how tired she'd been. There was no way she was wasting the night sleeping. She scooted off the bed and grabbed her shirt and underwear.

Jake got up and slipped on his jeans. "So, I kind of made plans for us."

"Plans?"

"Yeah, I want you to meet my brother and a couple close friends."

Elliot followed Jake out of the bedroom. This was really happening. She was going to meet his family. "Sounds like fun."

They walked into the kitchen. "Yeah, we're going to meet them at the bar Brian and I own." He grabbed two coffee cups and set them down by the coffee machine.

"I can't wait."

"Really?"

"Yeah, I want to see what Jake Quin was like before he became the rock star." Elliot sat down at the small dining table, and her eyes wandered over to a stack of papers.

Jake continued to work the coffee machine. "I must warn you. My brother can be judgmental at first, but he's going to love you. Dom and Chris will try to bust my balls like they always do. And Tom—"

"Jake, what is this?" Elliot stood as she grabbed the papers in her trembling hand. It wasn't like her to snoop, but the papers were out in clear sight, almost like Jake had wanted her to find them.

Shock spread across Jake's face as she shoved the papers at his chest. He clenched the documents, catching them before they fell to the floor. "Shit, Elle. I can explain."

"You're married?"

"It's complicated."

"Complicated?" Her voice shot up an octave the angrier she got. "Seems like a pretty simple yes or no answer to me." Elliot planted her hands on her hips, keeping them from causing bodily harm to Jake.

Jake rubbed his forehead, obviously worried about how she'd react to the answer. "Yes. I've been married for five years."

Elliot couldn't form the words she wanted to say. Hell, she didn't know what to say. She'd trusted him.

"I mean, we were married for less than twenty-four hours before she left me."

Elliot just stared at him, not knowing what to believe.

"I met this girl and lost my mind over her. I took her to Vegas and had Elvis marry us. The next morning, she was gone." Jake's gaze fell onto the floor. "God, this is embarrassing."

"I'd rather be embarrassed than be blindsided." She shook her head. "I was sleeping with a married man." Anger boiled in her veins. Right now, she couldn't stand the sight of Jake. "This is bullshit." The wall that guarded her heart was back up and stronger than ever.

She stormed out of the kitchen and headed toward the bedroom. No way was she sticking around for more lies.

"Elle, wait. It's not like that."

She whipped around. "Then tell me why it took you five years to divorce her?"

"I don't know."

"Not good enough. Not even close." She strode into the bedroom, finding her jeans on the floor. She picked them up and shoved one leg down the pant leg as she hobbled to keep her balance.

"Elle, sit down, and let's talk about this."

"No." Elliot zipped up her jeans and buttoned them. "I trusted you. I brought you into my life and introduced you to my son, and all along you were lying to me."

"To be honest, you never asked."

The glare she shot Jake was one of epic proportions, causing him to retract his remark. "I should have told you. I'm sorry." He followed her out of the bedroom. "Look, I don't know why I held on for so long. I was hurt and didn't understand why she left like she had. I had to prove to my brother that I hadn't fucked up again. Then, after a time, I had forgotten she even existed. I was on the road living my dream and loving you." Jake tossed the divorce papers on the end table. "The marriage was only on paper."

Elliot grabbed her bag from the couch and swung it over her shoulder. She met Jake's pleading gaze. She should have stuck to her guns and never got involved with the enemy. "Yeah, I'm sorry, too, Jake."

"Don't say that." The sincerity of his voice threatened her resolve to leave. She wanted to believe him. She tried to forgive, but she couldn't. He'd brought out the best in her, and now he'd taken it all away.

Elliot reached the door and turned the knob right before

tears rolled down her face. She kept walking down the hall as she heard Jake begging her to stay.

She skipped the elevator and went straight for the stairs to the parking garage. She threw her bag in the backseat of her car then got in, turning the ignition over. How could she have been such a fool? Elliot gripped the steering wheel as more tears fell. What was she going to do with her broken heart? She'd been betrayed by the one guy she'd never thought would.

a week later and Elliot still hadn't returned Jake's texts or calls. He was back in his old life, except he was the local drunk instead of tending the bar. Every day, as soon as the bar was open, Jake would head to the Tin Flask and order his poison for the day, bourbon on the rocks, stagger home, pass out, wake up, and do it all over again. Yeah, swimming in self-sorrow was pitiful, but Jake didn't care. He'd lost Elle.

Not even mailing off the divorce papers had brought him a brief moment of happiness.

"Isn't tomorrow the big announcement?" Brian asked as he cleaned a glass with his white terrycloth rag.

Jake looked up from his whiskey tumbler, surprised that his brother had remembered. He nodded.

"Don't you think you should go home and sober up?"

Jake tossed back the rest of his drink.

Brian slammed his hands on the table, gaining his attention. He leaned in toward Jake. "You're really starting to piss me off."

Through his drunken, bulletproof haze, Jake responded

with a slight slur. "Your face pisses me off." He slid his glass forward and motioned for another.

"You're cut off."

Jake sighed. He wasn't in the mood to have a go-around with big bro. He just wanted to be left alone, submerged in alcohol, until he was numb. Because being numb was a hell of a lot better than heartache. "Whatever. There's a liquor store down the street." With a stagger, Jake tried to get up from the chair. Shit, he'd had one too many.

"Keep your ass right there," Brian warned. "You're not going anywhere until I've said what's on my mind."

Jake was too far gone to object, so he kept his ass planted. "Well, go on. What brotherly advice do you have for me? Oh, wait, I know." He deepened his voice to mock Brian. "Jake, quit being a fuck up. Jake, everything you've done in life has been one big shit show." He shot Brian a cold glare. "Save your breath."

"That's not what I think at all, Jake."

That deserved an eye roll.

"Look, I don't know what happened while you were on the road. But I do know if you keep down this path, you'll ruin your life. Trust me, I know from experience."

Through his drunken haze, Jake didn't know if he'd heard him right. "What do you mean?"

"After Dad died, I fell into darkness and began drinking heavily. It took a lot of therapy to recover. I guess that's why I've been so hard on you, Jake. I don't want to see you go down the same path."

Jake felt like he'd been hit by a ton of lead. His brother had been an alcoholic, and he'd had no clue.

"I was a high-functioning drunk. I kept my drinking a secret. Not something I'm proud of." Brian busied himself cleaning the bar table. "Anyway, you can talk to me. No judgment here."

Jake didn't know how to process this. It didn't help that he was three sheets to the wind, and his brother's confession had him feeling truthful about his situation. "I wish you would have told me. I could've helped you."

"No, I needed to help myself first, and now I want to help you. What's going on, Jake?" Brian stopped scrubbing the tabletop and gave his little brother his full attention.

Jake exhaled. "I fucked up again. I fell in love with the enemy." God, he sounded like Elliot. "I fell for the lead guitarist who's auditioning for the same job as me."

"Are you insane?"

"I thought there was no judgment here."

Brian threw his hands up. "No judgment. Go on."

"Elliot's everything I could ever want in a woman and more. She's intelligent, beautiful, and the best damn guitar player I've ever heard. She's an amazing mother."

"She has a kid?"

"Yeah." For the first time all week, his lips curved into a smile. "Elijah. He's five and the coolest little dude."

"So, what happened?"

"I never told Elliot that I was married. She found the divorce papers lying on the table. I was going to tell her, but honestly, I had already forgotten about Stacy."

"Stacy served you with divorce papers? I thought you'd taken care of that before you left to go on tour?"

"Everything happened so fast. I didn't have time." And right now, he was kicking himself hard for not doing it. In his mind they'd been divorced, and the papers were just the formality.

"This is fixable."

Jake chuckled. "How? Elliot won't talk to me."

"You need to redeem yourself. Show Elliot that you love her."

"I don't know. Showering her with flowers doesn't seem right. Besides, she not into all that shit."

"Dig deeper."

Jake paused and thought about his brother's advice. Dig deeper? What did that mean?

"Sounds to me like you need a big sacrifice to show her that you mean business." Brian shrugged. "Think about it. But in the meantime, you need to sober up and get ready for tomorrow's meeting. Big things are on the horizon for you, little bro. All you have to do is grab it."

A sacrifice? Jake pondered the idea. There was one thing that would guarantee Elliot's happiness—Elijah's wellbeing. What could he do to ensure Elliot would never have to worry about her son's safety? What could he change to give Elliot more time with her son?

Like a lightning strike, an idea—an insane idea—came to mind. Jake shot off the barstool. His head hadn't been this clear in over a week. No matter the outcome of his plan, Elliot and Elijah would be happy. "Brian, you're a fucking genius."

Jake rushed out of the bar before Brian said another word. He pulled out his cellphone. It was still early enough to catch Joe at home. Jake hustled down the street to his apartment as he waited for Joe to pick up.

"Hey, dude," Joe answered. "What's up?"

"We need to talk."

22

*E*lliot sat in the lobby of Clef Tonic Records, waiting for Jill to arrive. The cozy, beige couch gave her no comfort as she prayed that she wouldn't run into Jake anytime soon. But it was unavoidable. They were meeting with Davidson, Joe, and Tyler to determine which one of them had made the cut.

She never looked back after leaving Jake's apartment a week ago. Preparing for today had been her primary focus. Heart be dammed, she was ready to fight tooth and nail for the job. This was her dream before she'd met Jake, and it was still her dream now. She wasn't ready to give up.

At least that's what she'd told herself to keep her mind off of Jake.

In all honesty, the nights had been hard. When the house was quiet, her thoughts drifted toward Jake. She missed him and questioned herself for not believing him or at least hearing him out. She blamed herself for the heartache, knowing better than to fall for another musician. But the bottom line always came back to the fact Jake had betrayed her; that was something she couldn't forgive.

The elevator door opened, and Jill walked in wearing her "here to kick ass" black dress suit. Her blonde hair was down and freshly blown out in large bouncy curls. "Phoenix," she beamed.

Elliot stood in time to catch Jill's hug.

"I'm so ready for this. Are you? I have a really good feeling."

Elliot wished she were as excited as Jill, but no matter how hard she tried to convince herself, she couldn't be. This didn't feel right. "Yeah." She faked a smile. "I can't wait."

Jill's excitement dulled as she looked her over. "What's wrong?"

"Nothing," Elliot lied. "What could possibly be wrong?"

Her manager eyed her suspiciously. "I'll let it go until after the meeting. We're going for drinks after."

"Elliot Phoenix," the receptionist called from behind the desk. "Davidson will see you now."

"Showtime." Jill flashed Elliot a bright smile, then headed down the hallway to Davidson's office. Elliot followed behind her, heart racing. Why was she so nervous? It was probably because she was about to see Jake.

Davidson greeted them at the door. Elliot caught the discrete googly eyes Davidson threw at Jill before they took a seat at a small table where Joe and Tyler were sitting. They acknowledged her and Jill with a head nod. Where was Jake?

Davidson pulled up a chair and sat next to Joe and across from her and Jill. Were they starting without Jake?

He shuffled a stack of papers she assumed was the contract. "Well, congratulations, Elliot Phoenix. You're Gracefall's new lead guitarist." He handed the documents over to Jill.

"Welcome to Gracefall," Joe added.

Jill looked over at her. "I told you. My gut is always right."

Elliot sprang out of the chair and hugged Jill. "I can't believe it."

"I'm so happy for you." Jill hugged her tight.

"Jake loves you, Elliot," Joe said, right to the point.

The celebration stopped, and Elliot turned to Joe. "What do you mean?"

"He conceded," Joe answered.

Elliot was stunned.

"He called me last night and said he was dropping out. Something about how being a session musician was more his style." Joe folded his arms on the table. "I call bullshit. What happened between you two?"

Elliot was still speechless.

"We want to hire you both, but the drama has us concerned," Davidson added.

"Drama?" Tyler exclaimed. "You're one to talk."

"You've got something you want to say?" Davidson shot the bass player a glare.

"Actually—"

"Enough," Joe growled. He turned to Elliot. "You need to find Jake and talk some sense into him. We need you both."

"Yeah, Elliot," Tyler added. "You and Jake have something special onstage. Gracefall needs that."

"Well, I need to give Big Rick an answer before nine p.m. If not, we're going with Elliot." Davidson stood, letting everyone know the meeting was over.

"Not so fast," Jill interrupted. "Why is it up to my client to bring back the competition? Jake's made his decision. This shouldn't be on Elliot's shoulders."

"Jill—" Elliot began.

"No." She held her finger up, shushing Elliot. "My client

has been more than reasonable with your lead singer being in rehab and the tour cancellation. If Jake left, then the job's solely Elliot's."

"Jill!" Elliot exclaimed.

"I'm sorry, but this is unprofessional."

"No, Sweetheart," Davidson interrupted. "It's rock and roll."

Elliot couldn't take any more of the arguing. Her head was spinning. Why had Jake thrown his dream away? This wasn't the way she'd envisioned getting the job.

Elliot stormed out of the office. She needed to find Jake. As she waited for the elevator, she called him. Straight to voicemail. "Shit!" Elliot paced in front of the silver doors. Where was Jake?

"Elliot!"

She looked up and saw Joe jogging down the hallway. "Hold on!"

As soon as Joe reached her, Elliot lost it. Tears streamed down her face. "I don't know where Jake is. He's not answering his phone. There's no way I can book a flight to Reno and get to Jake before nine. I don't even know where to start."

"Hey, calm down. I know where Jake's at."

Elliot froze. "Where?"

"He's here."

"What?"

"He called me last night telling me he was flying into Cali this morning and we needed to talk. That's where we were before the meeting with Davidson. He told me he wanted you to have the gig."

"Jake's here, in California?"

"Yep. He's staying at the Sunset Strip Plaza by The Black Veil."

That was only two blocks from here. "Joe Grace, you're a lifesaver."

"Wait."

Elliot turned back around.

"Jake gave up his dream so you could have yours. That's pretty fucking special."

The words lodged inside Elliot's throat as she held back the tears. "I know."

"Just bring Jake back. We need you both."

Elliot flashed Joe a grin. "Thank you."

Joe waved, motioning for her to get going.

The elevator door opened, and Elliot rushed in. The hotel wasn't far away; she prayed that she wasn't too late.

$\sim$

*E*lliot strode inside the hotel and headed straight for the check-in desk. As she waited, live music was playing from the lounge. The voice singing was familiar. She followed the music into a half-filled room and paused. Jake was sitting on a barstool, strumming an acoustic guitar in front of a microphone. He didn't notice her standing in the back of the room. She'd never seen a more handsome, sexy rocker. He took her breath away. His shaggy brown hair fell over his face, leaving the slightest glimpse of his nose and masculine jawline. Her knees went weak at the muscles in his arms straining against his black fitted T-shirt as he played. He was a rock star.

Jake looked up from his guitar and flicked his hair back. He sang into the microphone as he looked out to the audience. He saw her, and they locked eyes.

Jake sang.

"For the first time I'm right where I'm meant to be

Falling in love with you, my soul is full
Without you, I'm empty."

Tears welled in her eyes. No one had ever written a song for her; it was beautiful. Jake's voice was rich and smooth. The rhythm picked up as he went into the chorus.

"I'm doing time
For a crime I have committed
I'm doing time
For loving you
And I'll keep doing time until the day I die."

Every word he sang, she felt in her heart. She'd been wrong not to hear Jake out. He was giving up his dream for her, and she couldn't let that happen.

"Let me in
Let me mend what he has done
I see your scars of love
The bad and ugly, I'll take it all
No more chasing chaos; let's just be."

The song ended. Jake laid his guitar off to the side and walked off stage toward her.

God, she was a weeping mess. Elliot wiped her cheeks and took in a few deep breaths, pulling herself together, before Jake reached her.

"Hey." Jake shoved his hands in the front pockets of his jeans. "Did you like it?"

"What are you doing?" Her voice was low and a little shaky.

Jake looked behind him at the stage and then back to her. "My flight doesn't leave until tomorrow, so I thought I'd play some music."

Elliot shook her head. "That's not what I meant."

Jake exhaled. "I'm giving you what you and Elijah deserve."

"What about you, Jake?"

He shrugged. "I'll be fine knowing you and Eli will be happy."

"But this doesn't make me happy. I'm not taking the job unless you do." She folded her arms across her chest to let him know she was standing her ground.

"What do you mean?"

"The band wants to hire both of us."

Jake didn't say a word.

"No one has ever made such a sacrifice for me. I appreciate the kind gesture, but it's all or nothing. I can't think of another person that I want to share this experience with, and I won't do it without you."

Jake's expression was unreadable, and it drove her mad. "Please say something."

He pulled her into a much-needed hug. "Does this mean that you forgive me?"

Elliot swallowed past the lump in her throat and chuckled. "Yes, but no more secrets. I can't handle the drama."

"It's a deal." Jake took a step back. "I love you, Elle."

She looked up into his blue eyes and knew he was her forever. "I love you, Pretty Boy."

As she leaned in for a kiss, her cellphone rang in her back pocket. She looked at the number_Dax. "I have to take this."

Jake nodded and gave her privacy to take the call.

"Hello."

"It's Dax."

Elliot's heart sank. Why was he calling? She didn't need his shit today.

"I'm not filing for custody." His voice sounded grim. "I'm done fighting with you. Eli deserves to be with his mother."

She didn't know what to say. This wasn't like Dax at all. What was going on?

"I'll be gone for a few months. Maybe when I get back, I could see Eli? Supervised, of course."

"What's going on, Dax? Are you in trouble? Do you owe a drug dealer money?" Each thought heightened her concern. Yeah, she hated her ex, but she didn't wish him harm.

Dax laughed. "So, you still care."

"Barely." Elliot tamped down the urge to hang up.

"No, I don't owe anyone money. Let's just say I'm going on a long overdue vacation." Dax exhaled heavily as if he'd been defeated. "Tell Jake he won." With nothing else said, Dax hung up.

Confused, Elliot pocketed her phone and walked over to Jake. "That was Dax. He's not filing for custody."

"That's great!" Jake said, too enthusiastically.

Elliot planted her hands on her hips. "You wouldn't know why Dax would suddenly give up, would you?"

Jake shrugged. "Depends. Are you mad?"

She shook her head. "No secrets."

"I called in a favor from one of my cop buddies." Jake held up his hands before she could respond. "I know I shouldn't have, but I thought we were over, Elle. I couldn't let you go until I knew you and Elijah would be okay."

"Jake." She shook her head.

"Listen, all I know is they found a lot of drugs at his place, and they made a deal."

"What kind of deal?"

"Dax agreed not to file for custody and go to rehab instead of doing jail time."

Elliot was speechless. She didn't know if she was mad, relieved, or creeped out that Jake had gone that far.

Jake stepped closer and held her hands. She couldn't look at him because if she did, she'd fall apart. "Elle, I love you. I couldn't stand by and allow Dax to take advantage of you. You deserve better. Elijah deserves better. Please don't be mad."

"How could I be mad when you've written me a beautiful song?" A small laugh escaped her as she wiped a stray tear from her cheek. She looked up into his bright blue eyes. "I can't believe you did all this for me."

Strong hands framed her face. "You deserve to be happy."

It had been a long time since she'd been this happy. She had her career, she had Eli, and she had the love of a lifetime. Elliot leaned in and kissed Jake. "I love you, Pretty Boy."

EPILOGUE

Ninety days later
Tin Flask

Jake finished setting up Elliot's guitar on the small stage in the back of the Tin Flask. It wasn't like the tour stage setup with all the lights and pyrotechnics. It was simple, with an intimate ambiance, barstools, an oriental rug, and acoustic instruments. Nerves rattled him as he thought about tonight. His gaze set on the front door as he anticipated the arrival of his band members. Any minute they'd be walking in, ready to listen to a few songs he and Elliot had been working on while Dylan was in rehab. Jake hadn't seen them since he'd signed the contract three months ago. He still couldn't believe he was Gracefall's rhythm guitarist. His dream had come true. Better yet, he had Elliot to share the whole experience with.

Indeed, a celebration was due. Jake's divorce was final, Dylan was out of rehab, and he was finally free from the bar to live out his rock and roll dream. Brian hadn't been surprised when Jake had handed his half of the Tin Flask over. Jake actually felt like his brother was proud of him for pursuing his passion. For the first time, Jake was doing what he wanted to do. His father would've been proud.

Even the holidays had been perfect. Elliot and Eli had spent Thanksgiving with him, and he'd spent Christmas week at Elle's making everlasting memories of frosted sugar cookies and waking up Christmas morning with Elle in his arms. The last three months had been amazing, but he was missing the band. He was missing making music.

"Hey," Elliot greeted him with a kiss on the cheek. "Eli is all set with Mac, Sarah, and mom." Jake looked at the table next to the stage and smiled as he waved to the little dude. "Jill's running late." Elliot observed the bar. "And where the hell are the guys? Joe texted an hour ago and said that Mel and he were thirty minutes away. Tyler called and said he was at the hotel waiting on Dylan to decide on which pair of leather pants to wear." She rolled her eyes. "Such a diva."

Jake looked at his watch. He hoped the guys weren't blowing them off. Were they pissed because he and Elliot had been working on new material without them? It wasn't like they hadn't wanted to include them, but Jake thought everyone had needed time to cool off. Besides, working with Elliot had been unexpected. One night, they had been bored and began fooling around in the studio, soon realizing they worked really well together. His vocals and her guitar licks gelled together perfectly. So, yeah, they were stoked to introduce their songs to the band.

"Hey, mamacita." A chick with hair that was blue, fading into teal, twirled a drumstick in one hand and walked toward Elliot. "Are we going to get this thing started? Or are we being fashionably late?"

Jake and Elliot had bumped into Misti at the studio a couple months back. She'd been there laying down some drum tracks for the next Whiplash album. During one of Jake and Elliot's jam sessions, Misti had joined them. Who knew she also lived in Reno?

"Hey, girl." Elliot hugged her. "Looks like fashionably late."

"That's rock and roll." Misti walked behind her drum set and sat down. "Mind if I warm up?"

Jake was ready to respond when Misti responded for him. "Good." Her warmup started off slow and easy, then escalated into beautiful chaos.

"She's amazing," Jake said in awe as he and Elliot watched her play.

"Yeah, but she's no Joe Grace." Jake turned around, and Joe and Melody were standing behind him.

"Joe," Jake gave him a bro hug, then hugged Melody. "You guys made it."

"Of course," Melody said as she glared at Joe. "If someone would have asked for directions, we would have been here sooner."

"Woman, I told you I knew where I was going," Joe snapped back.

"Whatever you say, Rock Star." She shook her head.

"Oh, fuck yeah, dude!" Jake turned and saw Dylan and Tyler making their way to them.

Jake was taken aback at Dylan's appearance. He'd cut his hair short, his sunglasses were off, and he looked like he'd put on some weight. He walked with more confidence, if that was even possible. With just ninety days, Dylan was healthy. Jake couldn't be happier for him.

"Jakey." Dylan slapped him on the back.

Jake never thought he'd be so happy to be called Jakey. "Bro, how ya feeling?"

"You look amazing," Elliot added as she went in for a hug.

"I feel great." Dylan looked around the bar as if he was looking for someone. "Hey, Mellie, where's Dani?"

"She couldn't make it." Melody frowned. "She said something about having a hot date."

"Good for her." Dylan's smile seemed fake. "Hope it goes well."

Jake didn't miss the disappointment in Dylan voice. There was more to Dylan and Dani's relationship than the occasional booty call. Had he finally moved on from Ash? Dylan, always the mystery.

"Before we go on stage," Elliot changed the subject, "I have someone I want you guys to meet." She motioned for to Eli to join her.

Jake smiled as he watched her son innocently bounce over to Elle. God, he loved this little dude.

"Guys, this is my son, Elijah." Elliot rustled his shaggy blond hair.

"Holy shit. You have a son!" Dylan exclaimed.

"Dude!" Joe scolded. "Watch your language."

"Sorry, I'm shocked." Dylan looked at Eli then back to Elliot. "Thank God he looks like you."

Elliot smiled.

"Yeah, and he's a guitar shredder like his mom," Jake added.

"Hi, Elijah." Joe bent down. "I'm Joe." He held out his fist, and Eli bumped it. Joe shook out his hand as if the little guy had bumped him too hard. "No, he's a drummer."

Eli rocked from side-to-side, fidgeting. "Jake said guitar players get more chicks than drummers."

Jake froze as he felt Elliot's glare. "I swear I didn't say that."

"No, Jake's wrong, little man." Dylan put his hand on Eli's shoulder. "The front man gets all the chicks."

"Okay, Eli." Elliot placed her hands on her son's shoulders and turned him toward the table he'd been sitting at. "It's time to go back to Mac and Sarah." As Elliot headed back to the table, she shot the guys a playful glare over her shoulder.

"Well, that went well." Jake exhaled.

"What do you mean?" Tyler asked.

"Elliot was worried that you guys might think differently of her because she had a son."

"What?" Dylan exclaimed.

"Are you serious?" Joe said. "Why would we treat her any differently? God knows how many kids Tyler has out there."

Tyler's brows creased as if he was going to disagree, but then shrugged. "What I don't know won't hurt me."

The guys laughed, which lightened Jake's heart. With the band together again, it seemed just like old times. Everything in Jake's life was finally falling into place. He was playing the music he loved, he had the girl of his dreams by his side, and he'd won the respect of his brother. And Eli had been an unexpected, yet wonderful bonus.

"So, are you going to play us some music or stand around and play with yourself?" Dylan asked, pulling Jake back into his perfect reality.

Jake laughed. "Just stay out of trouble tonight, okay?"

About Victoria Zak

Victoria Zak is an internationally bestselling author of historical and contemporary romance. She weaves magic into her timeless tales, reminding readers anything is possible, especially with a dragon by your side. Raised in Dunedin, Florida, the sister city to Stirling, Scotland, no wonder she grew up fascinated with anything Scottish. Add the ocean into the mix, and it's easy to see where Victoria found inspiration for her stories.

As a child, she read anything she could get her hands on, which developed into full-scale book addiction by adulthood. Curious by nature, Victoria doesn't shy away from anything. She enjoys historical research and hanging out at the nearest coffee shop. Victoria currently resides in Maryland with her real-life heroes, her husband and two children.

Victoria loves to hear from her readers. You can connect with her through the links below:

www.victoriazakromance.com
victoria@victoriazakromance.com
Newsletter http://bit.ly/1uebjmR

facebook.com/VictoriaZakAuthor

bookbub.com/authors/victoria-zak

instagram.com/victoriazakromance

twitter.com/VictoriaZak2

BOOKS BY VICTORIA ZAK

Graceful: Vicious Love Tour Series

Rock Me to the Top

Rock the Line

Rocked and Bothered (2021)

Been Caught Rockin' (2022)

Guardians of Scotland Series:

Highland Burn

Highland Storm

Highland Fate

Highland Destiny

Highland Hope

Highland Unleashed (2022)

Ember Brooke Series:

Scorched Hearts

Hearts Under Fire

Daughters of Highland Darkness Series:

Beautiful Darkness

Deadly Darkness

Wicked Darkness

Stand Alones:

Once Upon a Winter Solstice

The Jewel of Grim Fortress

Midnight's Kiss